5-17-08

He couldn't get Jessica Parker out of his head.

Once again, her image flashed across Zach's mind. All buttoned up and drop-dead gorgeous.

Something stirred deep inside him, but he tamped down the sensation, shoving it far, far away.

He couldn't remember the last time a woman had turned his head, but he wasn't about to let Jessica Parker do so now.

He had to focus on his brother, on clearing Jim's name and shutting down the clinical trial. For that he needed Jessica Parker the scientist.

Zach had to ignore any unwanted thoughts about Jessica Parker the woman.

And he would.

KATHLEEN LONG

A NECESSARY RISK

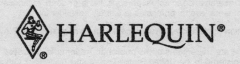

TORONTO • NEW YORK • LONDON
AMSTERDAM • PARIS • SYDNEY • HAMBURG
STOCKHOLM • ATHENS • TOKYO • MILAN • MADRID
PRAGUE • WARSAW • BUDAPEST • AUCKLAND

For Annie, the most unexpected—and wonderful—
blessing of my life. Thank you for reminding me that
dreams really do come true. I love you.

ISBN-13: 978-0-373-69243-9
ISBN-10:   0-373-69243-9

A NECESSARY RISK

Copyright © 2007 by Kathleen Long

www.eHarlequin.com

Printed in U.S.A.

ABOUT THE AUTHOR

After a career spent spinning words for clients ranging from corporate CEOs to talking fruits and vegetables, Kathleen now finds great joy spinning a world of fictional characters, places and plots. Having decided to pursue her writing goals when her first daughter taught her that life is short and dreams are for chasing, Kathleen is now an award-winning author of breathtaking romantic suspense for the Harlequin Intrigue line.

A RIO Award of Excellence winner and a National Readers Choice, Booksellers Best and Holt Medallion nominee, her greatest reward can be found in the letters and e-mails she receives from her readers. Nothing makes her happier than knowing one of her stories has provided a few hours of escape and enjoyment, offering a chance to forget about life for a little while.

Along with her husband, infant daughter and one very neurotic sheltie, Kathleen divides her time between suburban Philadelphia and the New Jersey seashore, where she can often be found hands on keyboard—bare toes in sand—spinning tales. After all, life doesn't get much better than that.

Please visit her at www.kathleenlong.com or drop her a line at P.O. Box 3864, Cherry Hill, NJ 08034.

Books by Kathleen Long

HARLEQUIN INTRIGUE
847—SILENT WARNING
914—WHEN A STRANGER CALLS
941—WITHOUT A DOUBT
959—RELUCTANT WITNESS
976—A NECESSARY RISK

CAST OF CHARACTERS

Jessica Parker—She's a lead researcher at New Horizon, a large clinical research facility. When the lifesaving drug trial under her supervision presents with dangerous side effects, will she accept the necessary risk, or will she fight to keep the drug from going on the market?

Zachary Thomas—His younger brother Jim committed suicide while a participant in the most recent Whitman Pharma drug trial. He's vowed to do whatever it takes to expose the truth—including tapping Jessica Parker.

Scott McLaughlin—He once led the Whitman Pharma trial before abruptly leaving the company. Was he falsifying study results, or is he a whistleblower with just the information Jessica and Zach need to expose the truth?

David Hansen—He's the holder of the magic key—the encoding information for the Whitman clinical trial. Will he help Jessica match the names of victims to participants, or will he alert the guilty parties that she needs to be silenced?

Miles Van Cleef—The head of New Horizon, he's dedicated his life to pursuing the safe and ethical development of new pharmaceuticals. But now he's faced with a tough choice—helping Jessica uncover the truth or doing whatever it takes to protect his company. Which will he choose?

Prologue

Jim Thomas pivoted slowly on one heel, frantically scanning the wall of his dorm room, searching for something—anything—familiar.

Framed photos assaulted his senses, distorted faces taunting, haunting. Their voices jockeyed for position inside his brain, screaming, threatening. He pressed his palms to either side of his head and squeezed.

Who were they?

Why wouldn't they stop?

His gaze landed on a calendar and he recognized his own handwriting. His room. He must be in his dorm room. Familiar surroundings. Safe.

Maybe the voices were a dream.

A very bad dream.

Maybe he'd wake up any moment now and the voices would be gone. The pain would be gone.

For a split second, a teasing sense of calm whispered through him before the unrelenting paranoia and dread took over once more.

Jim's chest ached and he struggled to draw in a breath, struggled to slow the racing beat of his heart. He opened his mouth to scream, but he couldn't speak, couldn't call out for help, his throat tight with fear and panic.

The pressure inside his head continued to build, becoming so intense he wished his brain would blow apart to end the agony.

Jim squeezed his hands harder against his skull and turned aimlessly. He bounced off the wall, then reached for the bed but staggered, losing his balance and slamming into the opposite wall.

He slid down the length of the cold plaster, fingers tracing the worn paint until they bumped up against the edge of the sliding glass door.

He sank to the floor momentarily but pulled himself up, using every ounce of strength in his body to will his legs to support his weight.

His heavy, bone-weary weight.

Heavy head.

Heavy heart.

Heavy life.

Jim sagged again but hooked one hand through the door handle, holding tight. The latch gave way and the door slid wide, opening to the pathetic patch of concrete the school called a private balcony.

He laughed through the pain, amazed he could remember the housing lottery, amazed how important winning this balcony had once seemed.

Now all he cared about was the pain.

The head-banging, excruciating pain that pulsated through his head. Minute after minute. Day after day.

The voices sounded again, urging him forward, promising him the pain would stop if only he listened.

He stumbled onto the balcony, welcoming the caress of the crisp autumn air against his face.

He gripped the railing and leaned over, studying the sidewalk below. The concrete drew a lazy pattern of curves through the carefully trimmed grass and the perfectly sculptured gardens. A group of students walking below laughed, no doubt consumed by the idiocy of college life.

They looked perfect. They sounded perfect.

Damned perfect.

Jim stepped up onto the bottom rail. First one foot. Then the other.

His headed pounded now as if his brain no longer fit inside his skull and pressed to break through. He looked to the sky and balanced, hoping the pain would ease. Hoping the pounding would stop.

But it never did.

The voices.

He had no choice now but to listen to the voices.

Jim stepped up onto the second rail and leaned forward, welcoming the rush of air against his face as he fell, arms spread wide.

He soared.

He flew.

He eagerly anticipated the imminent release from the pain, and as the ground rushed at him, Jim smiled.

At last.

Chapter One

Six weeks later

Nervous anticipation wound its way through Jessica Parker as she waited for Miles Van Cleef to introduce her to those gathered. She'd waited for this moment for a very long time. Years, to be precise.

Her newest promotion had been timed perfectly for today's media showcase. New Horizon held the event twice each year to tout their latest clinical trials and keep community support strong for their work.

She'd been named lead researcher on Whitman Pharma's testing of HC0815 two weeks earlier, and Van Cleef had asked her to handle one section of today's presentation.

She couldn't be more thrilled.

Or more nervous.

While she considered herself a whiz with facts and figures, people were another matter altogether. Let alone speaking in front of a crowd this large.

As Van Cleef covered the basics of New Horizon's relationship with area pharmaceutical companies and New Jersey College, Jess scanned the crowd, taking note of the expressions of those present.

Some intent. Some quite obviously watching the clock.

When her gaze landed on one individual in particular, she found herself riveted, unable to look away. Her typically strong intuition told her instantly something was amiss.

He didn't belong here.

His strong features showed no sign of emotion. Close-cropped dark hair neatly covered his head, and what had to be at least a three-day stubble graced the sharp line of his jaw.

While others in the room had shed their jackets due to the temperature inside the room, he wore a leather jacket yet showed no sign of perspiration.

No sign of weakness, actually.

She didn't need her advanced science degree to know he stuck out like a sore thumb. There was no doubt in her mind he didn't belong.

But who was he? And who was he with?

While the others present displayed an apparent interest—faked or not—in Dr. Van Cleef's presentation, taking notes and asking questions, the man in question did neither. He stared so intently at the presentation screen it was a wonder his gaze didn't sear a hole clean through the wall.

The appropriate media pass hung around his neck,

but Jess couldn't make out the name of the organization he represented, even though she squinted intently at the small square object.

Did he work for a competing institution? Had he gotten his hands on media credentials and crashed the showcase?

Investigational drug testing was a brutally competitive industry, and while they did their best to keep their work and specific details of their clients' drug development a secret, a breach in security was always a threat at New Horizon.

When the man's focus shifted unexpectedly to her, Jess looked away, her breath catching for a split second. She was being ridiculous, of course. He couldn't possibly know she'd been studying his every move—or lack thereof. And what if he did? She had a right to stare just as much as he did.

She turned her attention back to the presentation, waiting for her cue to approach the podium, but felt the man's eyes on her. She ignored the heat of his stare, focusing instead on the work here at New Horizon—specifically her work—and the comments she was about to make.

Taking over the Whitman Pharma testing had been a dream come true. While she'd been with New Horizon for the past two years, she'd spent the five years prior working in the New Jersey College medical research department. She'd learned firsthand just how miraculous today's medicines could be when it came to curing illness.

Excitement skittered through her as Van Cleef's presentation shifted to the topic of Whitman Pharma's development of a revolutionary treatment for Hepatitis C. At long last, a cure sat on the horizon—a total and complete cure. With none of the psychological side effects of existing drug therapies.

Jess wrapped her arms around herself and smiled. Wasn't this what every kid dreamed about? Being part of developing a lifesaving cure?

Today Hepatitis C. Perhaps tomorrow MS.

Her mind shifted quickly to her father's struggle, but she refocused immediately, not wanting to miss her signal to begin her talk.

Van Cleef called her name and Jess stood, winding her way between the row of chairs on stage as a smattering of polite applause filled the room.

She stole one last glance at the man in the leather jacket, her thoughts on finding cures evaporating into thin air when her eyes met his, still locked on her face.

Jess's stomach tilted inexplicably. Her warm smile slipped, yet the man's expression changed. One corner of his stern mouth lifted into a crooked smile, crinkling the skin around his dark eyes and softening the furrow that apparently had permanent residence between his brows.

She looked away, focusing on the podium and Dr. Van Cleef. The only thing she needed to worry about now was her presentation. She stole one last glance at the man as she arranged her notes before her, adjusting the microphone. Surprise slid through her when she found him making a notation on his pad, the first she'd seen him make all morning.

Yet her surprise was quickly replaced by unease when his dark stare lifted once more to her face.

Jess knew with certainty that any notation he'd made had nothing to do with New Horizon and everything to do with Jess herself.

But why?

If he was from the competition and he'd pegged her as an easy mark, he had another thing coming.

DETECTIVE ZACH THOMAS stared at the show before him, doing his best to contain the pent-up fury seething through every inch of his tense body.

New Horizon. The latest and greatest in conducting clinical trials for area pharmaceutical companies. And the last place his brother Jim had held down a job— albeit a very part-time position.

Clinical trial participant. *Healthy* clinical trial participant.

Zach shook his head, mentally berating himself for what had to be the millionth time since his younger brother's death. Why on earth had he encouraged Jim to take the job? For a bit of financial independence? For the contribution to science?

Damn.

Jim had been so excited. So thrilled to be helping test potentially lifesaving medicine and to be getting paid well for the work. He'd been alive.

So very alive.

And now he was gone.

Zach straightened in his seat, adjusting the blank tablet on his lap. All around him reporters made notations or whispered into handheld recording devices. If Zach cared about blending in, he'd do the same, but he had no desire to waste time writing down what were obviously practiced talking points.

If questioned, he'd explain he had a photographic memory. Hell, it was true, after all.

No matter what the coroner's report had concluded, there was a link between Jim's work for New Horizon and his death. Zach planned to do whatever it took to get to that truth.

He'd borrowed a buddy's press credentials to gain access to the new pharmaceutical testing company's open house, hoping to gain some insight into how the company worked, into who he might tap on the inside for information.

So far he hadn't spotted anyone who might be a potential target. The parade of staff had comprised hardened individuals. No one bearing the expression years of police work had taught Zach to zero in on. The open, curious, caring face.

Jim had been gone and buried for six weeks now. *Six.*

The kid hadn't lived to see his twenty-first birthday, yet here the New Horizon people sat bragging about their efforts to make the development and release of new drugs safe for the public at large.

Safe, his ass.

His younger brother had taken a header off the balcony after a supposed bout with depression and psychosis. The coroner had refused to call the death anything but suicide, but Zach knew better.

Jim hadn't been depressed or confused a day in his life, no matter what sort of statements his college buddies had given the officers on the case.

When Zach had pressed the investigating officers for their case notes, they'd told him to take care of himself, to leave the investigation to them.

When he'd tried to swipe those same notes from the files, the department had told him to take a hike.

After all, Zach wasn't stupid. He'd been around long enough to know how the game was played. Push hard enough, and sooner or later Internal Affairs would push back—straight to the department shrink and then straight to a paid leave.

Zach wasn't proud of what he'd done, but he also wasn't about to apologize for manipulating the system to his advantage—all the way to a three-month sabbatical.

More than enough time to investigate Jim's death and expose New Horizon.

The white-haired gentleman in a badly fitting suit—Van Cleef—continued to drone on, using a laser pointer to highlight features on a graph.

Zach sat back against his chair, patiently waiting for the next topic on the printed agenda.

The Whitman Pharma trial.

HC0815.

The drug that had taken Jim's life.

Zach swallowed down the ball of fury climbing up his throat and concentrated.

He studied the name listed as presenter for the HC0815 segment.

Jessica Parker.

He lifted his gaze back to the stage and scanned the faces of the scientists and number crunchers seated in the two rows of chairs.

He settled on a young blonde, her enthusiasm plastered across her face, and decided she was the best candidate to match the name.

Her sleek blond hair had been swept back off her face, no doubt into a tight bun or twist or whatever it was women called that style.

Her white lab coat was buttoned just about to her neck, exposing nothing other than a peek of flesh between the gentle curve of her chin and the collar.

Uptight, no doubt.

Yet when her eyes met his, the mix of emotions in her gaze was unmistakable.

Curiosity and a bit of nervousness.

His pulse kicked up a notch. If the woman was Jessica Parker, she'd be exactly the person he needed on the inside. She'd have the knowledge and the access to information his investigation required.

She also had the facial expression he'd been looking for. Open. Alert. Intelligent.

Her pink lips pressed into a tight line, and he immediately realized his attention had made her nervous.

Her pale blue eyes flashed back toward the podium and Dr. Van Cleef, as if she were waiting for her name to be called.

Perfect.

If she were Jessica Parker, he'd use his phony media credentials to cozy up to the woman, then drain her for every ounce of information she could provide.

Zach had been smart enough to keep a low profile after Jim's death. If he'd gone nuts and acted the role of grief-stricken older brother, he'd no doubt have been recognized today, bogus credentials or not.

Thankfully, he'd kept his head during the weeks since Jim's death. Hell, truth be told, there'd been a few days when he'd barely been able to lift his head from the pillow. He felt quite certain a large part of his heart and soul were permanently gone—destroyed in the seconds it took for his younger brother to plunge to his death.

The blonde stood and approached the microphone.

He smiled as he studied her, eagerly waiting to scrutinize every word she had to say.

Jessica Parker.

Zach had his mark.

Now all he had to do was wait for the right moment to make his move. When he did, he only had to remember one thing. His supposed identity.

Rick Levenson with the *Times Herald.*

Ms. Parker would never know what hit her.

Jess reached Dr. Van Cleef's side moments after he'd made his concluding remarks and was just about to begin the tour.

"I think we might have an impostor, sir."

Van Cleef smiled ever so slightly. "Leather jacket?"

Jess blinked yet realized she shouldn't be surprised Van Cleef had jumped to the same conclusion.

She nodded.

"I always liked your perceptiveness, Jessica." Van Cleef tipped his head toward the man, who appeared to be moving through the throng of reporters, headed directly toward where Jess and Van Cleef stood. "Why don't you show our guest some individual attention? Find out just what he's up to."

Jess had to admit she was less than thrilled with the idea, but she'd do whatever she could to protect the integrity of New Horizon's work.

She stole a quick glance at the approaching man, trepidation crawling across her skin.

"Will do, Dr. Van Cleef." She pasted on a smile. "My pleasure."

She stepped away from Van Cleef and pivoted, wanting to put herself in a position to appear casual when she approached the supposed reporter, but the man had already reached her side. She started momentarily but quickly gathered herself, smoothing down the front of her lab coat.

"Rick Levenson." The man extended his hand and smiled, the move not quite reaching his dark eyes.

"Jessica Parker." Jess gave his hand a quick pump

then took a backward step, wanting to put a bit of breathing room between them.

"I enjoyed your presentation on HC0815." He tipped his head toward the podium. "Fascinating possibilities."

Pride flirted with the cautious edge she'd snapped into place. "Lifesaving possibilities."

The man nodded. "No doubt. But at what risk?"

Jess shot him a frown. An odd question for a competitor to ask. Or was it?

"Pardon me?"

"The risk," he repeated, his dark gaze going steely and cold. "Just how much risk is justifiable in the development and testing of such a drug?"

She stiffened defensively. "The beauty of HC0815 is that it's virtually risk-free. The studies to date have shown none of the adverse mental reactions existing Hepatitis C drugs display."

Levenson held up one hand as if he'd heard enough. "I heard the company line during your presentation." He glanced toward the rest of the group, now headed toward the laboratory section of the facility, then he scanned the surrounding area. "Is there someplace a bit more private where I could ask you a few questions?"

Nervousness danced in Jess's stomach. "I really can't leave the group." Not exactly true yet not exactly false. No matter—she had zero intention of putting herself into an isolated position with this man.

There was something in his expression that wasn't

quite right. Something that went far deeper than a competitor or reporter's interest into how New Horizon was run and how HC0815 worked. For lack of a better term, she'd have to call the look in his gaze one of danger. A looming threat. It was as if he'd erected a wall of emotional control that could give way at any time.

"You can ask me any questions right here." She straightened. "Though I was quite forthcoming in my comments."

A muscle in his jaw pulsed.

Jess had a momentary vision of a coiled spring about to come apart.

"I'd like to hear the facts you kept out of your tidy remarks." His dark brows lifted toward his hairline.

Did the man think her a fool? "Who do you really work for, Mr. Levenson?"

He tapped the ID badge dangling from his neck. *"Times Herald."*

She shook her head in disbelief. "Well, then, if you're not out to steal company secrets, you must be looking for a sensational story where there is none."

He pursed his lips, an expression of pure confidence painting his features. "That so?"

She narrowed her gaze on him. "HC0815 is a groundbreaking drug, and the testing here at New Horizon leaves no room for sensationalism of any kind."

His dark eyes widened. "You sure about that?"

Jess stole a glance at the departing group, now out of earshot and very soon to be completely out of sight. Anxiousness edged through her system.

She pointed to the folder of media materials with which Levenson and every other media showcase attendee had been provided.

"Every bit of information you need is in the packet." She turned, fully intending to walk away. "I don't mean to be rude, but we need to rejoin the group now."

The man was obviously out to blast New Horizon in his paper. The less one-on-one time she provided him with, the better.

"So you know all there is to know about your clinical trial participants?"

Jess nodded, turning to face him. "What I don't know, I have access to. Their participation is randomized and coded for anonymity. Similarly, they're paid in cash. But I'm well versed with our results to date."

"Which are?"

"Stellar." She beamed. "This drug is going to save millions of lives."

"Even if it kills a few trial participants along the way?"

Every ounce of enthusiasm drained from Jess's body. Van Cleef had warned her about media reps being out for a sensational story. How sad that this man had chosen that tack and not a focus on how revolutionary the drug would be.

"I'm afraid I'm not interested in providing you with tomorrow's headline, Mr. Levenson." She turned back toward the group, now moving out of sight.

But Levenson's fingers brushed against her elbow as

she moved away. The momentary touch sent a jolt rocketing through her system.

"I'm not out for a headline."

When Jess spun to face the man again, the intensity of his expression stopped her cold.

"Are you aware of how many trial participants have died?" he asked.

Jess squinted at him. Was he insane?

"None. The safety results are spectacular." She jerked her head toward the group. "Shall we?"

"What about Jim Thomas, Ms. Parker? He jumped from a balcony after taking Whitman's drug. Did you log that side effect?"

Suicide?

Ice raced through Jess's veins, a sense of dread suddenly enveloping her and squeezing tight.

She'd heard of suicides during the trial periods for existing Hepatitis C medications, but HC0815? No. She'd certainly remember that detail.

"You must be mistaken. I don't remember a participant by that name—and I've reviewed every application and case report form completed to date."

Levenson stepped close. So close Jess was afraid he might hear how rapidly her heart beat in response to his allegation.

"I'd suggest you do a little digging." He dropped his voice so low she had to strain to hear him. "You might want to go back to the first trial for HC0815."

She frowned, shaking her head. "This is the first."

Levenson pursed his lips and gave her a wry grin. "For Hepatitis C, but rumor has it the same drug failed to gain approval for another usage."

Myriad thoughts whirled through Jess's brain. Surely Van Cleef would have told her if there had been an earlier failed attempt for FDA approval. He certainly would have brought her up to speed on any suicide during the current trial.

She shook her head. "You've gotten bad information from somewhere, Mr. Levenson. You might want to check your source."

He hesitated momentarily, and Jess thought she might finally have him backed into a corner. His next words shattered that illusion into countless pieces.

"I buried my brother last month, Ms. Parker. That particular suicide I can vouch for firsthand."

She shook her head again. "I don't remember a candidate with your surname."

"Thomas." The emotional strain in his voice had become evident. "Jim Thomas."

"I thought your name was Levenson?" Jess frowned.

The man pulled a business card from his pocket, handed it to her, then turned toward the exit. "I lied. Use the cell number when you're ready to talk."

Chapter Two

Zach headed across the New Horizon parking lot toward his restored Karmann Ghia, mentally berating himself as he walked. So much for keeping his cover intact. He'd told the blonde his true identity five minutes into their conversation—and he used the term *conversation* loosely.

He'd expected her to be more open to what he had to say, but she'd done nothing except tout the company lines about HC0815.

Revolutionary.

Lifesaving.

Risk-free.

He knew she was wrong, knew it just as strongly as he knew he needed air to breathe. No clinical trial company should be allowed to get away with changing study results, and apparently that was exactly what New Horizon had become involved with. If the company was doing whatever it took to keep their multimillion-dollar-accounts and keep their pharmaceutical company clients happy, they had to be stopped.

And Zach was just the man to do so.

The Little Brother consumer watchdog group had contacted him at Jim's funeral. Zach had thought their timing left a lot to be desired, but everything they'd said jibed with what his gut had been screaming.

HC0815 was the reason his brother was dead. The drug caused psychosis in a number of otherwise healthy clinical trial participants, and now one had died. Jim.

Zach's heart squeezed as he dropped into the driver's seat.

His brother deserved better than what he'd gotten. Far better.

Their parents had been killed in a multivehicle car accident when Jim was only thirteen and Zach twenty-six. Zach had spent the past seven years trying to be the mother and father Jim had lost. They'd mourned together, moved forward together and embraced life together.

They'd celebrated—and how—when Jim graduated from high school and got accepted by New Jersey College. They'd found student loans and Zach had scrimped and saved. He'd done whatever he could to ensure Jim got the education he deserved.

The New Horizon HC0815 trial had seemed too good to be true. High pay for taking a revolutionary and safe drug. Animal testing had shown no side effects. The same was expected in humans.

Zach had actually encouraged Jim's participation, delighted the kid was so proud of what he was doing.

What a fool he'd been.

If he could spare one other family the loss he'd suffered—save one other kid from a drug-induced suicide—he would.

And Jessica Parker would help. Whether she wanted to or not.

He'd gotten over his surprise at her initial reaction. Of course she'd been defensive. She wouldn't be a loyal employee if she hadn't been. But once she dug into the New Horizon database and found out he was telling the truth, she'd come around. She had a light in her eyes that hinted at ethics, and ethics were exactly what he needed right now.

He'd tipped his hand by offering the information on the previous trial—a withdrawn application by Whitman Pharma for the treatment of pancreatic cancer. The law protected the company, allowing them to claim whatever information the trial had provided as a trade secret.

Yet, even if there had been a cover-up, the data must exist somewhere.

Finding that data was Zach's next step.

If he could provide concrete evidence Jim's suicide hadn't been the only one linked to taking the drug, he'd be on his way to putting an end to the testing.

He pulled out of the New Horizon parking lot and into the midday Princeton traffic.

Jessica Parker.

Her image flashed across Zach's mind. All buttoned up and drop-dead gorgeous.

Something stirred deep inside him, but he tamped down the sensation, shoving it far, far away.

He couldn't remember the last time a woman had turned his head, but he wasn't about to let Jessica Parker do so now.

He had to focus on Jim, on clearing Jim's name and on shutting down HC0815. For that, he needed Jessica Parker the scientist.

Zach had to ignore any unwanted thoughts about Jessica Parker, the woman.

And he would.

JESS DROPPED HER FOCUS to the name on the card.

Detective Zachary Thomas.

She lifted her attention to the man's retreating back, dread dancing up and down her spine.

Suicide?

During the current HC0815 trial?

And during a past trial she'd never heard about?

As Zach Thomas rounded the corner and disappeared from her sight, Jess turned, not toward the media showcase tour but toward a different section of the facility. The section no one but security-cleared staff could access.

She had questions that needed answers and ghosts that needed exorcising.

HC0815 was now *her* baby, her responsibility, and she intended to make sure nothing stopped the revolutionary drug from making it to the public.

Especially not random allegations tossed around by a grief-stricken detective.

How dare he crash the media showcase by impersonating a reporter? The nerve of the man. Yet sympathy tugged at her heart, twisting ever so slowly. The man had lost his brother. She needed to remember that, as much as she wanted to wring his neck for voicing such lies about their work.

But *were* they lies?

She swiped her ID badge through the panel outside the lab, pushing the door open once the buzzer sounded.

If Thomas's allegations weren't lies, then she'd been kept completely in the dark about the existence of a previous trial, one that had been stopped for an unknown reason. She'd known Miles Van Cleef long enough to know he was a forthright and honest man. He'd never do such a thing. But what if he had been kept in the dark, as well?

Was it possible?

And what about the current trial?

Her predecessor, Scott McLaughlin, had beaten a hasty departure from his position as head of the HC0815 trial. At the time, Jess had written off his action as an aggressive career move, but now she wondered.

Had he stumbled upon something and been forced out?

Jess settled in front of her computer terminal and pulled up the list of archived databases, refocusing on the possibility of a previous study. There were none. But then, the trial may very well have been run under a different name.

She searched on Whitman Pharma and came up with three previous trials, all for drugs which had successfully made it to market and not one with an indication for pancreatic cancer.

She blew out a sigh and sank back against her chair, relief easing the tension that had gripped her every muscle since she'd met Detective Thomas.

Someone had given the man bad information about prior suicides. But what about that of his brother?

She pulled up the current study, knowing full well each participant's identity would be coded and anonymous, but any adverse reactions should be logged, especially one involving psychosis. She carefully scanned the list of participant numbers and results, tracing her finger along the column for implications.

No suicides.

Not one.

No depressions.

No anxiety or panic disorders.

HC0815 truly was the wonder drug they'd all pinned their hopes on, completely free of psychological side effects.

She needed a list of participant names to put her mind at ease and she knew just where to start.

The file of hard-copy applications from potential candidates.

Jess moved toward the opposite side of the lab, using her key to open the locked file drawer. It was company policy to retain all applications, even for those individuals not selected.

The data was also computerized, but—call her old-fashioned—Jess wanted to review the actual forms on the off chance Jim Thomas's information hadn't been entered into the system.

Several minutes later she'd flipped through every single form, scanning each applicant's name.

No Jim Thomas.

Detective Thomas had been certain his brother had taken part in the trial. Perhaps he'd misunderstood or perhaps his brother had lied.

She slipped his business card from her pocket and studied it. He deserved to know he was operating on false assumptions.

Jess reached for the lab phone but stopped. She needed to speak with Miles Van Cleef before she made any contact with Thomas.

Knowing the media showcase should be long over, she pushed out of her seat and headed for the man's office, more than ready to put this entire episode behind her.

"I CAN ONLY GIVE YOU A minute, I'm afraid." Van Cleef spoke without looking up from the jumbled mess of papers on top of his desk.

Jess never ceased to be amazed someone so brilliant could be so unorganized, even though the man was able to put his fingertips to whatever he needed without a second thought. Perhaps his clutter was actually a physical manifestation of his brilliance.

Jess shook off the random thought and refocused on the reason she'd asked Van Cleef for the meeting. She stood behind the chair opposite his desk rather than sitting.

"I thought you should know why the gentleman in the leather jacket was actually here."

"Ah." Van Cleef lifted his gaze. "How did your detective work go?"

Funny he should choose the word *detective*.

Jess hesitated for a split second, then plunged in. She summarized Thomas's allegation regarding the earlier failed trial, watching as color fired in Van Cleef's neck and face.

No wonder. He was more passionate about the integrity of New Horizon's work than anyone. She'd known he wouldn't take Thomas's claims lightly, but he had to be made aware the rumors were floating in the public.

"The results of the prior trial are inconsequential to the current testing."

Van Cleef's words hit Jess like a ton of bricks.

Prior trial?

Had Thomas been right? And if so, where was the data?

"When I accepted this new position, I wasn't informed HC0815 had been through prior trials."

"Trial," Van Cleef corrected. "As in one and one only. A complete disaster for a variety of reasons, most of them having to do with Whitman Pharma's withdrawal of the product from the FDA approval process."

Jess's head spun with questions. "Why is there nothing in the database?"

Van Cleef shook his head, his wire-rimmed glasses sitting crooked as usual. "No reason to keep information on products that don't gain approval."

"But what if the trial exposed a risk to patients? What if the data presented safety implications for the Hepatitis C indication?"

Her question captured Van Cleef's attention completely. The man visibly tensed. "The drug was pulled by Whitman. It's not for you or me to question why." He frowned, his expression intense, serious. "Ancient history. You're paid to stay on top of the current Whitman clinical trial, not worry about the past. Have there been any alarming side effects to date?"

"None documented." Jess shook her head, debating whether or not to tell Van Cleef the rest of the conversation.

She drew in a deep breath, hesitating.

"If that's all, Jessica, I really do need to get back to work. The media showcase set me back hours, as usual."

"The detective claims there's been a suicide in the current trial."

Van Cleef's white brows snapped together. "That's preposterous."

"His younger brother," Jessica continued. "A supposedly healthy candidate. He jumped from his dormitory balcony after allegedly taking HC0815."

"I'm assuming you've already checked the records? The case report forms?"

Jess nodded. "No record of a Jim Thomas in the applications. No record of a suicide in the results."

"There you have it." Van Cleef nodded, then refocused on his work, dismissing her with this move. "Your detective is mistaken. End of story."

But as Jessica headed back toward her work area, she couldn't shake the memory of Detective Thomas's determination. His was the face of a man who knew what he was talking about—or at least was fully convinced he was telling the truth.

In addition, she couldn't remember ever being dismissed so abruptly by Van Cleef. Was he hiding something? Was he trying to brush off her questions?

She hated to think so, hated that the idea had crossed her mind, but now that it had, she had to see her questions through. It was how she was wired.

On the off chance there might be information that had been purged from the records and databases, she had to locate the one person who might have had access to, and knowledge of, additional information.

Scott McLaughlin. He might have left New Horizon, but the guy had a mind like a steel trap. If he'd ever seen data from the previous trial or reviewed Jim Thomas's application for the current trial, he'd remember.

Now all Jess had to do was convince the man to talk.

ZACH LEANED OVER HIS kitchen table and scrubbed a hand across his face. Disgust and anger fought for position in his gut as he reread the local newspaper article covering Jim's death.

His brother, never one to seek the spotlight, would have hated the attention. Even more importantly, he would have hated the implication he'd committed suicide because he'd grown weak mentally.

Weak.

Not the Jim Zach had known all his life.

Zach sank into a battered kitchen chair and spread the pieces of the puzzle across the table. The article. The notes from the investigation. The list of friends who had detailed Jim's downward spiral.

He traced a finger across each of the investigational notes, all in his handwriting, all recreated from memory after one quick glimpse of the department files.

He stopped his hand when his fingertips brushed against a short stack of paper. Hard copies of the e-mails from Jim detailing the start of the semester and his work with New Horizon.

Zach's heart grew heavy in his chest.

He had to admit his brother's tone had changed in the days before his death. Zach should have realized something was wrong, should have done something. Anything.

The familiar guilt edged through his system. He did nothing to shove the sensation away. Hell, he deserved to feel guilty. He'd failed the younger brother who had looked up to him as he would a parent.

Zach had let Jim down.

It was that simple.

He drew in a deep breath then blew it out slowly, bolstering his determination. He might have let Jim down in life, but he wasn't about to let him down in death.

He'd start at the beginning and work this case harder than he'd ever worked another case. This time it was his brother's memory he'd fight to vindicate.

Zach pulled a writing tablet from the far side of the table and listed the evidence he'd gathered so far.

Testimony from friends.

E-mails from Jim.

Prior Whitman Pharma clinical trial information from consumer watchdog group.

He shook his head and squeezed his eyes shut momentarily. There wasn't much to go on, and the first item on the list pointed to Jim's declining mental state.

As Zach saw it, he needed concrete proof of two things—Jim's involvement in the HC0815 trial and data from the previous Whitman Pharma drug study.

Jim had reported to the hospital affiliated with the college for his daily dose of HC0815, so there had been nothing in his personal effects to link him to the drug trial. And the only thing the Little Brother watchdog group had been able to provide regarding the earlier Whitman drug study was hearsay.

Zach needed far more in order to prove New Horizon and Whitman Pharma's guilt and take them down.

He swept all of the papers to one side, frustration

growing inside him as he ran the conversation with Jessica Parker through his head for what had to be the hundredth time since that afternoon.

Jessica Parker.

The key to unlocking the evidence Zach needed. The key to getting inside New Horizon.

While he'd like to think it possible to investigate without the woman, the truth was he needed her cooperation.

As Zach shoved the newspaper article and the investigative notes back into the manila envelope where he kept them, he flashed once more on Parker and her defense of New Horizon.

Earning the woman's trust wasn't going to be easy, but it was a necessity.

Now, all he had to do was figure out a way how.

JESS FINGERED THE business card in her jacket pocket as she walked from her car to her condo, revisiting the day's events in her head.

She'd stayed at New Horizon even later than she normally did, and the heaviness of the impending night pressed against the fading sun. The late hour had also forced her to park farther away than she liked.

She'd left a message for Scott McLaughlin at his home number but hadn't heard back from him. She'd decided against calling Detective Thomas. At least for now.

Once Scott confirmed what Van Cleef had said, Jess would break it to Thomas that he was operating under false pretense and his brother's mental illness had been just that—and not the by-product of the clinical trial.

She turned the corner toward her street, passing the alley that ran behind the neighborhood grocery market. The small hairs at the base of her neck pricked to attention, and she mentally chastised herself.

The alley had given her the creeps since the day she'd moved in. It didn't help that her favorite pastime was devouring one romantic suspense novel after the other late at night.

Her imagination was no doubt working overtime.

When movement sounded from behind her, she glanced over her shoulder, half expecting to see an attacker closing fast.

Instead she saw nothing. No one.

"Get a grip, Parker."

She quickened her pace nonetheless, practically breaking into a jog as she approached the last intersection before her building. She came to a quick stop, looked both ways and moaned inwardly as a battered old Cadillac approached at a snail's pace.

The widow Murphy. The bane of the neighborhood pedestrian. The woman should have lost her license years ago, yet still she drove. The problem was you never knew if she was going to be driving fast or slow…or both.

As if on cue, the car sped up, zipping past Jess in a blur.

Thank goodness she hadn't made a move to cross the street.

She'd been so focused on Murphy's car, Jess hadn't sensed the presence behind her, but she sensed it now.

A footfall sounded. Several paces back, if she wasn't mistaken.

Jess's pulse began to race, and she squeezed her eyes shut momentarily, trying to calm herself, trying to think rationally.

She was merely on edge from sneaking around the lab and the files. Not her usual MO.

Logically speaking, it would make sense for another pedestrian to be on the street. After all, the October weather hadn't yet turned terribly cold and the evening promised to be clear and beautiful.

Another footstep sounded, and Jess turned to offer a greeting, deciding to face her ridiculous fear head-on.

Her breath caught at the sight behind her. The sidewalk stood empty. Yet she'd heard the footfalls. *That* she hadn't imagined. No way.

Something moved beyond the stand of small maples the town had planted during its beautification project. A shadow. A shape.

A man?

Jess wasn't about to wait to find out. She pivoted to face the street, breathing a sigh of relief when she spotted no oncoming traffic in either direction.

She sprinted across, heading straight for her condominium complex, not daring to steal another glance over her shoulder. Not wanting to risk the slightest slowing of her pace.

As she reached the steps to her building, the sound of someone running behind her was unmistakable. She'd be a fool to punch in her security code and risk whoever followed gaining entrance to her otherwise secure condo. She'd rather face her pursuer head-on, screaming for help in the open.

Hers was a close neighborhood, and she had no doubt help would be with her in no time flat, if needed.

The footfalls slowed as they neared, and Jess turned, doing her best to mentally prepare for whatever—and whoever—she might find behind her.

A middle-aged man stood close yet kept a respectable distance. His complexion was scarred, as if he'd battled severe acne in his youth. His dark hair had begun to recede, and he'd slicked it back, creating a stereotypical New Jersey tough-guy appearance. His manner of dress, however, belied his intimidating looks.

He wore an impeccable suit, crisp white shirt and tightly knotted tie. His clothes showed not a hint of wear or wrinkling, as if he'd just dressed or emerged from a corporate limo.

He reeked of money and confidence, and Jess didn't recognize him from the neighborhood.

"Can I help you?" she asked, hoping the fear that had her trembling inside wouldn't infiltrate her voice.

The man tipped his head to one side, a slow smile lifting the corners of his mouth. "I was going to ask you the same thing."

Jess narrowed her gaze, suspicion filtering through

her. "I'm fine. You're not from around here, are you? Do you need directions?"

He pursed his lips. "You were running. What made you do that?"

You, she thought.

The man's tone had turned icy, and Jess swallowed reflexively, doing her best to ignore the fingers of dread that wrapped themselves around her neck and squeezed.

The man took a step toward where she stood, but Jess held her ground, steeling herself.

"I was wondering if you had reason to be afraid of something." His voice dropped low now, menacing, the implied threat unmistakable.

She shook her head. "Why would I be afraid?"

He leaned near and Jess seriously considered screaming. She tensed, ready to strike out should he make a move.

"Sometimes people stumble into situations where they don't belong," the man continued. "You'd be surprised what can happen to a person who loses her way, to those she loves, especially when they can't defend themselves."

Jess fought the urge to take a swing at him but stood frozen to the spot. She hated how much fear his words had shot into her system. Just who was he threatening? Her? Her family? Her disabled father?

The man tipped his chin, then pivoted away from her. "Take care now. And don't forget to lock your doors. You wouldn't want to leave yourself vulnerable."

Jess did nothing. Said nothing. She merely stood and

watched him walk away as if her feet had been anchored in concrete.

Either the man was merely a Good Samaritan with a penchant for gloom and doom or he'd followed her with the express intent to intimidate.

She'd put her money on the latter.

Someone had sent the man with the message for her. She'd stumbled onto something someone else didn't want her to stumble upon. But what?

Detective Thomas's allegations were the only development out of the ordinary in her otherwise predictable life. Surely Dr. Van Cleef hadn't sent the well-dressed man out to scare her. And other than those two, the only person she'd contacted was Scott, yet she'd mentioned no specifics in her voice mail, purposely being discreet.

Could the conversation she'd just had have been a random warning from a well-meaning stranger?

When she punched in her security code and entered the building, she had her answer. The door to her condo sat wide-open, as if she'd gone off to work and never pulled it shut behind her.

She stood to the side of the threshold and listened but heard nothing. Glancing inside, it was evident nothing obvious had been touched or moved. The condo was designed as an open loft, and she was able to scan the full interior from the door.

Her living area, kitchen and sleeping area were all as she'd left them with no intruder in sight.

No matter. Jess knew she'd locked the door just as

she knew someone was sending her a message. No doubt the man she'd just encountered on the street.

She pulled her cell phone from her briefcase and speed-dialed her parents' number. After they'd assured her they were fine, she disconnected, prepared to call the police. Then she had an even better thought.

She pictured Zach Thomas's dark and intense features, a shiver tracing its way across her shoulders at the image. What if the detective was behind both the intrusion into her apartment and the warning from the stranger? What if he'd orchestrated the moves to intimidate her into cooperating?

Her gut told Jess he hadn't, but there was only one way to find out.

She pulled Detective Thomas's card from her pocket, read the digits of his phone number, then punched them into her cell.

Thomas's gruff response suggested he did not appreciate the interruption.

Too bad.

"Detective Thomas?"

"Who is this?"

"Jessica Parker. We need to talk."

Chapter Three

Zach sat uncomfortably on the edge of Jessica Parker's sofa, still angered by the woman's accusations but thankful for the excuse to speak to her again so soon.

She drew in a slow breath, and for a split second worry clearly shone through her controlled features. She squinted, as if his presence made her terribly uncomfortable.

Zach pinned her with a glare. "It's not every day I get accused of sending some thug to threaten a woman and break into her apartment."

"I thought you might have done it to get me to cooperate with you. To get me to pull the data."

Heat fired in Zach's face, and he knew he was treading a thin line when it came to control. He might be desperate to get to the truth, but even he wouldn't go so far as intimidation. Would he?

"Lady, I'm a police officer. The last thing I need to do is scare you into believing me. I've got the facts on my side."

She shook her head. "I'm not so sure you do." Her eyes locked with his, their intensity shaking him to the core. "Your brother's name is nowhere to be found in any of the records." She spoke flatly, her gaze never leaving Zach's. "Could he have lied about his involvement?"

Zach battled to keep his sudden anger and frustration under control. He shook his head. "My brother was not a liar."

She gave a quick lift and drop of her shoulders.

"What about the earlier study?" he asked.

Hope simmered inside him as she nodded her head.

"Dr. Van Cleef said an earlier trial did take place, but Whitman pulled the drug out of the approval process."

He arched one brow. So she'd asked. "My information was right, then."

Jessica shook her head. "There's no data. No proof of any adverse reactions."

Zach shoved a hand through his hair. "Why else would they pull the drug?"

"Competition, insufficient market potential—"

"Someone has to know something, remember something," Zach interrupted, lifting his gaze to hers, momentarily transfixed by her pale blue eyes. He gave himself a mental shake and refocused. "Have any ideas?"

Jessica sucked in a deep breath, then sighed, turning toward her phone. "I do, actually. Scott McLaughlin. I replaced him as lead researcher on HC0815. He left rather abruptly."

"Any reason why?"

She shook her head as she flipped through a small spiral book. "We were only told he was gone. He had a terrific reputation, though. Let me try him again."

"You've already tried?"

Zach had to silently admit his surprise. So he'd piqued the woman's curiosity enough that she'd put out feelers to the former lead researcher.

Jessica nodded. "Before I left work."

"Anyone else you talked to other than McLaughlin and Van Cleef?"

"No one. And I left a vague message for Scott. No specifics."

Zach listened as she left another message for McLaughlin. The woman appeared calm and collected, but the slight tremor in her hands gave her away.

The man who'd approached her outside had scared her more deeply than she was willing to admit.

Zach had reached her upscale condominium less than thirty minutes after her call. The odd sense of protectiveness that had surged through his every muscle lingered still, unnerving him, something very few things in life did.

He'd examined the lock on her front door and noted no sign of forced entry, yet he believed her story, believed she'd locked up before she'd gone to work that morning.

If nothing else, hers was not the sort of personality that forgot to lock doors. Far from it.

He studied the condo as she continued to speak into the phone, noting the precise order and lean decorations.

No. Jessica Parker was not a woman who would ever leave a door unlocked. If anything, Zach had been surprised she didn't have better security.

Whoever had gained entrance was a pro. Of that Zach had no doubt.

"That was his cell phone," Jessica said as she replaced the receiver, then tucked a stray hair behind her ear. "Maybe he'll pick up that message."

"And your earlier call?"

"To his home." Jessica hesitated momentarily. "At least I think so."

He nodded, standing to face her head-on. "Could anyone have overheard you?"

Could they? Jess wondered. It was a definite possibility.

"I suppose." She gave a quick shrug. "But I didn't uncover a thing."

Zach Thomas's dark gaze grew steely and intense. "Don't you think that's enough? The fact you looked— the fact you asked questions—might be enough to put someone on the defensive."

"Perhaps." Jessica took her time, choosing her next words carefully.

She'd pulled the online news archives after she'd called the detective. She'd read the stories about Jim Thomas's mysterious suicide. According to witnesses, he had been depressed, but based on the data back at the lab, HC0815 would have had nothing to do with it.

"You need to prepare yourself for the very real possibility your brother was *not* a participant," she continued.

Thomas's dark brows snapped together just as the phone rang.

Jess snatched it from the receiver, breathing a sigh of relief when Scott McLaughlin's voice sounded over the line.

"I have a fairly good idea why you called," he said.

"Really?" Jess answered, a bit taken aback by the matter-of-fact tone of McLaughlin's statement.

"Did you find the bogus HC0815 data I coded?"

His words stole her breath away. "Bogus?"

The man's chuckle filtered through the phone. "Maybe *altered* is a better term."

Silence beat between them.

"Look, I thought I'd be able to sleep at night after I quit. I was wrong. I need to come clean, Jess. Any interest in hearing what I have to say?"

Her heart slapped against her ribs, and she nodded, as if Scott could see the move.

"You alone in this?" Scott asked, not waiting for her answer to his previous question.

Jess stared at Detective Thomas, wondering what Scott's reaction would be to his involvement. "There's a detective. He's got a few theories he wants to chase down."

"Game on." McLaughlin's voice dropped low. "Just name the time and the place."

ZACH WAITED, SITTING in a strategically selected booth at the Bordentown Diner.

Back to wall. Face to diner entrance.

He glanced at his watch.

McLaughlin was already nine minutes late. Not a good sign.

If the guy had chickened out, their chances of uncovering the trade-secret trial results and any altered HC0815 data would fall onto Jessica's shoulders. Somehow Zach couldn't picture her hacking into the New Horizon system.

She might be scared right now. She might be intrigued. But was she dedicated enough to the cause to risk her job? Risk the integrity of the company she worked for?

Beyond that, her family had been threatened. There was no telling at what point the woman might bail on the entire investigation.

Zach slid a sideways glance toward the counter across the room from where he sat. Jessica sat with her profile to him, long blond hair swept into a ponytail and tucked into a ball cap.

Even in blue jeans and a faded sweatshirt, she was a beauty. No doubt about it. Yet the severe set of her slender jaw and the intensity of her gaze told anyone who cared to notice that she kept herself protected and closed off.

Zach supposed most scientific types might be the same way, focused solely on their work, but he suspected Jessica Parker's demons went a bit deeper than a desire to crunch data.

No matter. He wasn't here to contemplate the

woman's emotional state. He was only here to use her for whatever information she might be able to access regarding HC0815 and the role it had played in Jim's death.

If Zach could expose New Horizon and Whitman Pharma, he would. He'd make sure no other *healthy candidate* developed a sudden urge to take a swan dive off a balcony or rooftop.

Jessica looked at him over her shoulder, and he frowned, gesturing with his eyes for her to turn around and concentrate on the coffee cup in front of her, not on him.

The worried glint in her eye was a sharp reminder of reality. She might have her emotional walls soundly in place, yet someone had followed her, threatened her, threatened her family.

Why? Simply because she'd asked questions of Van Cleef? But who? Van Cleef himself? Hardly. The man didn't look capable of harming a fly. Someone else on the inside? Perhaps whoever had instructed McLaughlin to tamper with trial data and outcomes?

Or had Whitman Pharma stepped in to make sure no one and nothing jeopardized the billions of dollars they stood to earn once HC0815 gained FDA approval and hit the market?

A disheveled man with jet-black hair stepped through the diner entrance, cutting off Zach's thoughts. Tall and lean, he looked to be no more than thirty years old. And he looked nervous as hell.

McLaughlin, Zach thought. Had to be McLaughlin.

The young man moved slowly through the diner, bypassing the hostess as he did so. He held nothing in his hands. No papers. No folders. No disks.

Damn.

Zach had hoped today's meeting would provide concrete evidence—physical proof. Unless he had a secret compartment in the battered T-shirt and jeans he wore, McLaughlin had decided otherwise.

He moved toward where Zach sat, and Zach nodded.

McLaughlin stopped next to the table.

"Great day for the race," Zach said, repeating the line they'd agreed upon.

McLaughlin dropped into the opposite side of the booth and wiped at his upper lip.

If the guy was this nervous due to a simple meeting, he'd never hold up under intense pressure or under questioning.

Zach shook off the thought, signaling to the waitress. Based on the sharp angles of McLaughlin's face, there might be one way to get him to relax and to earn his trust.

Food.

ZACH WAITED UNTIL McLaughlin had inhaled the plate of eggs and bacon before he launched into his questions on HC0815.

At first mention of the clinical trial, McLaughlin stiffened, yet his bloodshot eyes brightened.

"You know, I loved that job," he said, features tensing.

"Then why'd you leave?" Zach prodded.

McLaughlin smiled ruefully. "I think you already

know that answer or you wouldn't have had Jess make contact with me."

"Jess contacted you on her own," Zach replied.

"Then why isn't she sitting with us?" McLaughlin asked.

Zach answered only with a frown.

McLaughlin jerked a thumb toward the counter. "She's pretty hard to miss. I spotted her before I spotted you."

Damn.

If McLaughlin had spotted her that easily, chances were anyone who might be watching had done the same. They'd have to be far more careful from here on out.

Though, if McLaughlin could provide cold, hard evidence, Zach's probe might be over much sooner than anticipated.

"She's already had threats. It's better this way."

The genuine surprise that registered on McLaughlin's face let Zach mentally check the man off the list of possible suspects in Jessica's break-in and threat.

McLaughlin glanced at the clock on the wall. "Let's get to it, shall we?"

Zach gave a tight nod.

"There was an earlier trial for a pancreatic cancer indication for HC0815. Whitman pulled the drug from the approval process, but not until after two trial participants died."

Adrenaline zinged to life in Zach's veins. So the Little Brother watchdog group's information had been correct. "Suicide?"

McLaughlin nodded. "With no prior history of mental illness."

Anger tapped at the base of Zach's skull. "How can Whitman get away with keeping two deaths quiet?"

"Trade-secret rule." McLaughlin's lips thinned. "The big pharmaceutical boys know how to protect themselves."

"What about the current trial?" Zach asked.

McLaughlin took a sip of his coffee and nodded. "There's already been trouble." He tensed. "The powers that be instructed me to eliminate the evidence or else."

"Do you have proof?"

"Of who was behind the order?" McLaughlin shook his head. "Whoever it was paid me handsomely and anonymously—in cash. I'm not proud of what I did."

"What about the case report forms?"

McLaughlin nodded. "They're still in the system, I just protected the access." He narrowed his gaze. "You act like you already knew about the latest adverse reactions."

Zach nodded his head, saying nothing.

McLaughlin's narrow gaze widened. "*Thomas.* Holy...I should have made the connection. How?"

"Brother," Zach replied in response to McLaughlin's verbal shorthand.

McLaughlin blinked. "I'm sorry, man. So sorry."

Zach leaned forward across the narrow table. "So you understand why proof is so important to me."

The other man nodded. "For a while there I thought you might be a reporter yanking Jess's chain, but now I get it. You're out for revenge." He smiled as if pleased.

If thinking Zach wanted revenge made the man talk, so be it. Zach could play whatever part the investigation required him to play.

McLaughlin shot a nervous glance around the diner. "You know about the other suicides?"

"You just told me. From the earlier trial."

McLaughlin leaned forward, disbelief crinkling the skin around his tired-looking eyes. "No. The other suicides from this trial."

"The current HC0815?" Zach's pulse kicked up a notch.

"Two other students," McLaughlin answered. "One, a month before your brother. One, the week I left New Horizon."

Zach couldn't believe McLaughlin's words. So Jim's hadn't been the only death? Two others had died, one as recently as three weeks ago, and the media hadn't gotten wind of it? But how?

"Whitman Pharma." McLaughlin answered Zach's unspoken question. "Lots of money and lots of spin control. Don't think clinical trial data isn't manipulated every day." He arched his brows and smiled bitterly. "It is. The almighty dollar is just that—almighty."

McLaughlin pushed away from the booth. "I'd better get going. I'll get the codes and access instructions to Jess."

"Why'd you do it?" Zach asked as the other man stood.

"We all have our vices," McLaughlin answered, his features going flat. "And our demons."

Zach shook his hand, then watched him leave, mulling over his parting words.

At first, when Zach spotted the dark van racing down the street, his mind refused to wrap itself around the likelihood of what was about to happen.

But when McLaughlin dodged to get out of the way and the van swerved toward him, reality sank into Zach's brain.

A split second later McLaughlin was hit.

JESS WATCHED IN HORROR as a dark van came seemingly out of nowhere. The vehicle struck Scott at a high speed, tossing his body onto the hood and against the windshield like a rag doll.

Glass shattered, and Scott's body fell to the asphalt like a discarded piece of trash as the van sped away.

Horrified passersby rushed to Scott's side and Jess leaped to her feet, pushing away from the counter. Several other diners rushed toward the door. She could only pray there was a doctor or emergency worker in the group.

Poor Scott was going to need all the medical assistance he could get.

Zach was at her side in an instant, his grip tight on her elbow. She spun on him, struggling to pull her arm free, to get to Scott. "What are you doing?" Fear and anger heavily tinged her tone.

"Stopping you before you do something stupid like run out into the open."

His dark features seemed even more intense and closed off than usual. Jess hadn't thought it possible.

"I have to help him." Her voice wavered with emotion as she choked out the next words. "He's here because of me. That van came out of nowhere."

She looked to the scene outside, where one man stooped down, fingers to Scott's neck. He looked up at the others gathered and shook his head.

Zach kept his grip on her arm yet squeezed gently. The uncharacteristic move sent surprise skittering through her.

"There's nothing we can do to help him." Zach's eyes narrowed, softening at the corners. "I need to get you out of here."

"But what if—"

Zach pressed his lips into a tight line and shook his head. "He's gone, Jess. And I intend to make sure whoever did this to Scott doesn't do the same thing to you."

Fear edged up against her shock. "Me?"

A look of disbelief washed across Zach's dark eyes. "You don't honestly think this was a random accident, do you?"

Did she?

She'd like to think it was, but her logical mind wouldn't allow her the luxury. Someone had wanted Scott silenced—and they'd succeeded.

If whoever had been behind the wheel of that van had spotted her in the diner, her life might be in danger. If they knew Scott had been meeting with Zach, his life might be in danger. Not to mention the warning she'd been given about her parents.

Jess shifted her focus back to Zach. His stare hadn't wavered from her face. She did her best to shove the fear she felt from her mind. Similarly, she compartmentalized her shock and sadness at Scott's brutal death until she could process the emotions later on.

Zach was right. They had to get out of there, had to leave Scott behind. "Let's go."

Jess had promised herself she wouldn't trust Zach Thomas, but at this particular moment, trusting the man appeared to be her only option.

Heaven help her.

Chapter Four

An awkward silence hung heavily in the living room of Zach's house.

He sat on a battered leather recliner, elbows on knees, face in palms. On occasion, he stole a glance at Jessica, furrowed his brows then returned his stare to the hard-wood floor.

A knot of fury hung at the back of his throat, having lodged there the moment he watched McLaughlin get mowed down and eliminated as if he'd never existed.

Guilt assaulted Zach's every sense. McLaughlin had been at the diner because of his investigation, because of Jessica's phone call. Had whoever hit McLaughlin followed the man to the restaurant? Or had his killer known he'd be there based on watching—or listening to—Jessica?

Zach refused to let his brain so much as consider the possibility the hit-and-run had been an accident. He'd been around too long to be that naive. He knew a hit when he saw one.

Scott McLaughlin's death had been murder—a purposeful, well-executed murder.

Someone had wanted the man silenced before he could provide additional information on HC0815. There was no doubt in Zach's mind.

Zach lifted his gaze once more to watch Jessica. The flush that had colored her cheeks as they'd fled the diner had faded. Her pale complexion and huge blue eyes served as stark reminders of the horror she'd just witnessed.

She'd shoved the sleeves of her sweatshirt to her elbows and sat cross-legged on Zach's sofa, clutching an embroidered pillow to her stomach. She hadn't said a word since they'd entered the house, and Zach was beginning to worry about shock.

"We should have done something." Jess's soft words broke through the wall of silence that had separated them ever since they'd made the decision to come here, knowing her apartment might not be safe.

Zach studied Jessica's expression. The innocent look of fear in her gaze, the determined set of her jaw. The woman was a study in contrasts. Hard yet soft. Frightened yet fearless.

He shook his head. "There was nothing to do. Let the police sort it out."

Her pale brows lifted toward her hairline. "Aren't you the police?"

Zach shook his head. "Not for the next three months." He pinned her with a gaze he hoped would convey his desire to cut off this particular line of questioning. No such luck.

"What is that supposed to mean?"

He sat silent for a moment, deciding how much to tell the woman.

When he spoke, he did so slowly, deliberately. "I'm not in agreement with their findings on my brother's death, and Internal Affairs made it clear I'm to let this go."

"They suspended you?" She straightened.

"Not yet." He shook his head, then shrugged. "I'm just a man on sabbatical looking to finger the persons responsible for killing my brother."

"And if innocent lives suffer along the way?"

The woman didn't pull any punches. The harshness of her words left Zach momentarily speechless, pulling the guilt he already felt closer to the surface. He shoved the emotion away.

"I'm trying to *save* innocent lives. Remember?" Zach shook his head. "Whoever drove that car is responsible for your friend's death. Not me."

But deep inside him, Zach's gut protested his words, knowing full well his actions had played a role in McLaughlin's death.

He pushed himself out of the recliner, scrubbing a hand across his face. He was beginning to sound defensive. Better to walk away before the conversation continued. "I'll make some coffee. We've got a game plan to figure out."

As he passed Jessica he pulled a well-worn quilt from the back of another chair and tossed it into her lap. "Wrap up in that. You're too pale."

He ignored the look of surprise that registered on her face as he pushed through the door to the kitchen and shifted his every thought away from what had just happened toward what needed to happen.

He had to get his hands on the data from the failed trial and he had to find another way into the New Horizon database—quickly. McLaughlin had mentioned two additional suicides. Zach planned to talk to their families, their friends.

The questioning was necessary, but his gut knew what he'd find. Two students who had never before shown a single symptom of depression or psychosis. Two students whose lives had been healthy and carefree.

Two students whose worlds had turned into ticking time bombs the moment they made the decision to serve as participants in the HC0815 trial.

JESSICA WATCHED ZACH'S retreating back as he pushed through a swinging door separating the living area from his kitchen. She pulled the quilt tightly to her chest, surprised by the kind gesture. She hadn't thought the man capable.

Instead of wrapping the soft material around her, she stood, heading for the small fireplace on the far side of the living room and the mantel lined with framed photos.

The frames were no-nonsense, much like Zach himself. Black lacquer mixed with the occasional silver. Simple. Free of all ornamentation.

The photos inside the frames were another matter altogether.

In one shot, Zach smiled brightly, his features alive and full of joy. He'd hooked one arm around a teenager's neck. Jim Thomas, no doubt.

Zach and Jim shared identical smiles, their features a combination of the couple that stood to the side of the pair in the photo, watching the scene.

Their parents?

The ages seemed right. Zach looked to be at least ten years younger in the shot than he was now.

When had the news article said his parents had been killed? Seven years earlier?

Jess scanned the remaining photos. Most of them of the teenager, chronicling his life as he grew into a man.

The two brothers obviously had been close—and happy. Each picture of Zach hinted at a sincere joy Jess had yet to see mirrored in his features.

The Zach Thomas she knew bore little resemblance to the smiling man in the photographs. He didn't seem capable of caring about anything except taking down her company.

Jess scanned the frames one more time, looking for one additional thing. Another female. She didn't know why it mattered, but suddenly it did. She wanted to know everything about Zach's life—his family, his work, his loves. She wanted to understand him. She needed to understand him.

The man's theories stood to threaten everything she'd worked for in the testing of HC0815. She at least wanted to know what made Zach Thomas tick.

Her second scan of the photos found not a single other woman besides the person Jess presumed to be Zach's mother. Did he have no one in his life? Or had he simply chosen to keep any evidence of a love life hidden away somewhere in a less public area of his home?

Jess snapped her thoughts away from Zach and his life and refocused on the face of Zach's brother.

Jim Thomas.

Her heart ached. The young man appeared to have had his whole life ahead of him. Had his involvement in the HC0815 trial played a role in his tragic death? Or had he been on a crash course with a preexisting mental illness he'd successfully hidden from his brother?

Was Scott right in what he'd said? Had other lives been lost as a direct result of the Whitman trial? She had to find out—had to know. She'd devoted her life to scientific study, to the search for the truth. Because that truth threatened her very work was no reason to ignore the possibility.

She needed to find out exactly what Scott had been talking about. She had to get inside the New Horizon database. Whatever it took.

"He was a great kid." Zach's voice interrupted her thoughts, his tone tight, forced.

"I'm sorry for your loss," Jess answered. She pointed to the shot of the brothers and the couple. "Your parents?"

He nodded without saying a word, extending a mug of coffee in her direction.

Jess took the hint, not pressing him for additional information. Instead she took the mug, returned to her seat on the sofa and pulled the quilt tightly around her lap.

She'd suddenly grown cold, chilled by the possibility everything Zach had theorized might be true.

"I need to get inside the database," she said.

"Preaching to the choir." He sank back into his chair and fixed her with a determined stare. "I have another idea of where to start—"

"The suicides?" she interrupted before he'd finished talking.

One dark eyebrow lifted, apparently impressed with the leap her mind had taken. He nodded.

"How will we find them?" Jess asked. "There were no records of suicides in the files. None."

Zach pressed his lips into a tight line. "I've got a buddy at the *Times Herald* who will be happy to tap into the county medical examiner's files for me."

Jess sat back, remembering Zach's phony identification at the media showcase.

"Rick Levenson?"

He nodded.

Now she was impressed. She hadn't even considered searching death records. "How long will that take?"

Zach pulled his cell phone out of his pocket and flipped it open. "We're about to find out."

JESS PULLED INTO HER parents' drive a few hours later. She and Zach had agreed to meet at the Sunrise Diner the next morning. The restaurant was far enough out of town that they shouldn't be spotted.

Zach had insisted on returning to Jess's condo with her, checking every closet and window before she convinced him she was safe.

She'd been a nervous wreck after he left, just the same. As much as she'd wanted to take a shower to wash off the memory of Scott's face as he was struck down, the thought of being inside the shower while whoever had killed Scott was out there somewhere kept her dry and dressed.

Her parents' front door sat unlocked when she tried the handle. She winced. They had to start taking precautions, whether they liked it or not.

If Jess was a target, so were they. Anyone who knew Jess's background knew her greatest vulnerability was her love for her father.

"Mom? Dad?" she called out as she shut and locked the door behind her.

"Living room, honey," her mother answered.

A twinge of guilt filtered through Jess when she rounded the corner from the center hall and spotted the lines of fatigue framing her father's eyes. She'd called two hours earlier, and her dad had no doubt been sitting up in his wheelchair since her call. He hated for visitors—especially Jessica—to see him lying in bed, but sitting in his chair wore him out.

"I'm sorry it took me so long to get here." She did her best not to project how much it broke her heart to see her father like this—how much she hated the disease that had taken away the strong, vibrant man she'd idolized her entire life.

Her father gave her a dismissive frown and a slight shake of his head. "Not long at all," he answered.

"Coffee, honey?" her mother asked. "Tea? Water?"

Jessica shook her head. "No, thanks. I really just need your advice on something."

She sank onto her parents' sofa, next to her mother, and leaned toward her father, placing one hand on his knee.

"Do you remember when I called you last night after the break-in at my apartment?"

Her mother nodded and her father blinked his eyes.

"I may have gotten myself in over my head with something."

As both her mother's and her father's gazes widened, Jess proceeded to bring them up to date on everything that had happened, from her first conversation with Detective Thomas to watching Scott die outside the diner.

"The man outside my condo threatened those I love," she said in conclusion, lifting her eyes to her meet her father's worried gaze. "Chasing down this theory might put your lives in danger. I'll walk away from it right now if you want me to."

"We can take care of ourselves," her mother answered.

"These people have to be stopped." Her father's words rang strong and sure.

Jess realized, not for the first time, that his disease might have taken away his physical strength but it hadn't touched her father's soul, his spirit.

She voiced the question out loud that had been haunting her since she'd first met Zach Thomas. "What if this wasn't a drug for Hepatitis C? What if it was a cure for MS?" Jess shook her head. "I'm not proud of what I'm about to say, but I'm not sure how far I'd go to see you walk again, Dad. I'm not sure what study outcomes I'd hide if it meant helping you."

Stunned by her own admission, she looked into her father's eyes. "What constitutes a necessary risk?"

Her father's lip curved into a slight smile. "My mobility isn't worth a single life, Jessica. I think you know that." He drew in a breath, fighting through his obvious fatigue. "If people are dying and if Whitman is doing something to hide that, you've got to fight them."

He paused, working to form his words. "Seems to me they're not focused on the cure. They're focused on the profit. Detective Thomas is right."

"But what about the threats? I won't put you two in danger." She tipped her chin toward her parents.

Her father's forehead wrinkled, and her mother pressed her lips into a tight line.

"We've got a security system," her mother answered. "We know how to use it." She drew in a deep breath, then released it. "You do as we raised you, dear. You do the right thing."

But even as Jessica settled into her old bedroom later that evening, a jumble of thoughts and possibilities battled for position inside her mind.

After all, Zach Thomas might be totally wrong about the HC0815 trial. She might be worrying for nothing.

Jess shook her head and sank onto the soft mattress. She knew better.

People didn't break into condos, deliver threats and commit murder without reason.

Detective Thomas was right. Something was very, very wrong at New Horizon. Now all they had to do was find out what…and by whom.

Jess's gaze landed on the clippings and photos that covered her old bulletin board. She pushed up off the bed and crossed the room, resting her chin and palms atop a well-loved chest of drawers.

She studied the photos of her family—shots of Jess and her father before the multiple sclerosis had stolen away his mobility inch by inch, limb by limb.

She smiled at a photo of the two of them posed after a long day of fishing, nothing dangling from their lines except a pair of discarded sneakers they'd plucked from a local lake.

In a second picture, her father stood next to her, one arm wrapped around her shoulder as she held up a tennis trophy.

Tears blurred her vision, and she let them fall, too tired to blink or wipe them away.

Her father had always been so proud. So encouraging.

As Jess flicked off the bedroom lamp and crawled into bed, lowering her head to the pillow and settling into the lumpy mattress, she realized her father had worn that same look tonight.

Proud. Encouraging.

He expected her to do the right thing.

He'd raised her to do the right thing.

And she would.

She'd do whatever it took to get to the bottom of what was really happening to the HC0815 trial participants. She had to. They were her responsibility.

Not exposing the truth was a risk she was no longer willing to take.

ZACH LOCKED HIS GAZE on the Parker house, focused on the one remaining sign of activity—the glow of light from a single double-hung window on the second floor.

The room where Jessica stayed, no doubt.

When he looked away, he did so just long enough to stretch his neck or pour another mug of bitter coffee from his Thermos. He kept careful vigil of the street, studying each car that drove past, though there hadn't been many.

Jessica's childhood neighborhood was apparently safe and quiet, untouched by the kind of violence Zach saw every day closer to the city—the violence that had done its best to turn him dead and cold inside after all these years.

He flashed on the image of Scott McLaughlin lying broken in the street and shuddered.

If Jessica had been previously untouched by violence, that illusion had been shattered today. The woman had been visibly shaken. Visibly stunned.

Zach couldn't say the same. While he'd felt responsible for bringing McLaughlin to the diner, Zach had felt oddly detached from the crime itself.

He swallowed and scrubbed a hand across his face.

Maybe the violence had finally won. Maybe he'd been exposed to so much death and hatred that the cold had succeeded in setting up permanent residence in the hollows of his bones and limbs.

Zach had spent his entire career fighting to stay alive inside, fighting to keep the daily horrors of his job at bay. The moment he'd gotten the call about Jim he'd lost the will to fight. The cold had won.

Even though Zach believed he and Jessica had a real shot of blowing Whitman Pharma and New Horizon off the map, he wasn't sure he had it in him to force the cold back out again.

Maybe he was better off this way.

Perhaps it would be easier to go forward in life with the unemotional edge work—and life—had brought him.

The glow from inside the upstairs window winked out, and Zach wondered just what it was Jessica had been doing. Working? Reminiscing? Evaluating the pieces of the puzzle?

She didn't strike Zach as much of a sentimentalist, so he found it hard to believe she'd spent the evening sorting through shoe boxes of treasured high school memories. More likely she'd spent the time charting out the possibilities for all the reasons why New Horizon was not at fault in his brother's death and the other suicides.

The woman was a poster child for corporate loyalty. She'd been shaken by McLaughlin's death, but he had a feeling that, given time, her desire to bring the so-called, lifesaving HC0815 to market would win out over any of Zach's theories.

All the more reason he needed the names of the other two suicide victims. If their stories mirrored Jim's, Jessica Parker would be forced to face reality. Somewhere inside the sainted New Horizon process, a vital step had been compromised.

Zach drew in a deep breath and leaned back against the driver's seat, closing his eyes, refocusing himself on the task at hand. Proving Jim's suicide had been nothing short of murder.

And making the responsible party—or parties—pay with everything they had.

The pink glow of daybreak was edging through the sky when Zach's cell phone jolted him from sleep.

Damn. How long had he been out? He stole a glance at the Parker driveway as he answered his phone. Jessica's hybrid still sat parked to the side of her parents' garage.

Zach breathed a sigh of relief.

"Thomas," he barked into the phone, hoping he sounded more alert than he felt.

"Sleeping on the job again?" The teasing lilt of Rick Levenson's voice brought the slightest lift of a grin to the corners of Zach's mouth.

"No, I thought I'd try going undercover as one of you lazy investigative reporter types."

Rick's chuckle filtered across the line before he spoke. "Well, while you were napping, I was digging up two names for you."

Zach straightened, coming fully awake and alert. "Ready."

"Are you writing this down?" Rick asked.

Zach grinned, knowing full well Rick knew about his exceptional memory skills. "What do you think?"

A sharp burst of laughter sounded in Zach's ear. "Your mind's a scary place, Thomas. Scary."

"You have no idea."

Levenson laughed once more, then cleared his throat, his tone going serious. "Amelia Grant and Roger Kowicki." Silence beat across the line, then he continued, the taunting lilt returning to his voice. "How high are you willing to go for the addresses?"

Anticipation began to spread through Zach, the familiar rush of moving forward with a case and new clues. "A dozen Boston creams," he said without thought, having had this particular exchange with Rick too many times to count. "Not a doughnut more."

Levenson sighed dramatically. "You drive a hard bargain."

Zach silently repeated the addresses to himself as Rick rattled them off.

"Let me know if you need anything else," Levenson said after he'd finished delivering the information.

"Will do." Zach hesitated for a second—and only a second—knowing his next statement might insult his friend but had to be voiced nonetheless. "I probably don't need to tell you—"

"This conversation never happened," Rick interrupted. "No worries. Just be careful out there."

"Thanks. You'll be the first to know when something breaks."

Zach disconnected the call and reached for the Thermos. His stomach rolled at the prospect of downing more coffee, but he needed a quick shot of caffeine before heading home to shower for his meeting with Jessica.

Surprise edged through him when Jessica emerged from her parents' house a split second later, literally at the crack of dawn.

She wore the same jeans and sweatshirt she'd worn the day before, only her long blond hair tumbled about her shoulders, gleaming in the rosy morning light.

He swallowed, doing his best to ignore the undeniable attraction he'd begun to feel for the woman. He gave himself a mental shake.

He needed Jessica Parker for her connection to New Horizon. Nothing more. The last complication he needed was a physical attraction, an emotional weakness. Once she'd pinned up her hair and donned her lab coat, he'd no doubt lose any hint of the attraction simmering inside him at this moment.

It was seeing Jessica's softer, more human side that had thrown him momentarily.

His wayward thoughts weren't anything a decent meal and a day full of interviews wouldn't cure.

The brake lights illuminated on Jessica's car, and she began to back the vehicle toward the street. Zach cranked on the Karmann Ghia's engine and waited.

They weren't supposed to meet for another two hours, but there was no time like the present to kick their investigation into high gear.

Chapter Five

Jess had no sooner pulled out of her parents' driveway than a navy Karmann Ghia moved to block her path.

Fear seized at her throat and, for a tenuous moment, time stood still. Then she saw the driver's face.

Zach's face.

Adrenaline drained from her every muscle. How could she not have recognized his car?

Jess pulled to the side of the road and lowered her window. Zach had already climbed out of his vehicle and was headed her way.

What on earth was he doing here? And had he been here all night?

Watching?

Waiting?

Standing guard?

The relief that flooded through her at the sight of the man unnerved her, scared her. She was becoming too reliant on the sense of security Detective Thomas inspired, whether he'd been the impetus for her current situation or not.

All her adult life Jess had prided herself on being independent, free of any emotional ties except those to her parents. Yet here she stood, two days after her initial encounter with Zach, comforted by the man's mere presence.

She needed to get a grip.

"Were you here all night?" She asked the question before Zach could utter a word.

He made a show of shaking his head. "Thought this would be my best bet to find you when you weren't home."

She narrowed her eyes on him, suspicion sliding through her. "You came looking for me at this time of the morning?"

He nodded. "New info." Zach tipped his chin toward her parents' house. "Everything all right in there?"

Was everything all right?

Jess had the sudden urge to tell him about her father's physical condition, but she resisted. Her personal life and that of her family was none of Detective Thomas's business.

"Fine," she answered flatly. "Just fine. They weren't worried about the threat. My mother says they've got a security system in place."

Zach nodded, frowning a bit. "We could hire private security to cover nights."

Jess's stomach gave a slight twist at the thought.

Private security.

What on earth had she gotten herself—and her parents—into?

"Jess?"

She started a bit at the intrusion of Zach's voice. "Let me think on that."

She gave one last look at her parents' house. Her mother. Her father. Her life.

If things got too hot, she'd step aside. She had to.

Her parents' lives weren't a risk she was willing to take.

Jess turned to Zach, noting the dark stubble covering the sharp line of his jaw and the downward turn of his tired eyes. He might claim he hadn't slept here all night, but he certainly didn't appear to have gone home.

"What's so important that you tracked me here?" She squinted at him. "I thought we were meeting in a couple hours."

"Follow me now and I'll tell you." He stepped away from her window and reached for his driver's door. "Coffee's on me."

JESS AND ZACH SAT quietly as the waitress brought their breakfast. She was anxious to hear what was so important it couldn't wait, but he'd wanted to hold off on their discussion until they'd be clear of interruptions from the waitress.

In the meantime, they'd sat drinking their coffee. Zach had kept his focus on the parking lot, avoiding Jess completely, while Jess had spent her time studying the man himself.

She couldn't help but stare at the way fatigue softened Zach's features. She'd found him attractive before—in a rough-and-tumble I'm-all-man-and-don't-you-forget-it sort of way—but now…now he appeared more real, as if a bit of his hard edge had slipped.

She wasn't altogether sure she liked the way that realization made her feel.

"Their names are Amelia Grant and Roger Kowicki," Zach said abruptly as he dug into a heaping serving of scrambled eggs, sausage and home fries.

Jess had settled for a fruit salad and cottage cheese, and now found her mouth watering at the decadent spread covering the man's plate.

He glanced at her quickly, the intensity of his stare sending a shiver down her spine.

"The other two suicides," Zach added, as if she wouldn't know what he was talking about.

Jess forked a large piece of cantaloupe into her mouth, chewing thoughtfully before she spoke.

"Do we know which schools they attended?"

Zach shook his head, swallowing a mouthful of coffee. "Just addresses. Parents' addresses."

Jess brightened. "So we'll start by calling them? Then what? Ask them point-blank if they've ever heard of HC0815?"

Another shake of his close-cropped hair. "Element of surprise. The drop-in. Always a smart move."

She frowned. "But it's not as if they're under suspicion for anything. Why wouldn't you at least call to give them a heads-up we're on our way?"

"Too much time." Another huge forkful of eggs. When was the last time the man had eaten? "We've got a better shot at getting something useful if they don't have time to think about things before we get there."

She supposed Zach's words made sense. Still, her sensibilities screamed at the thought of pulling a drop-in on two families deep in mourning.

"Are they local?"

Zach nodded.

Suddenly Jess realized she was far behind in the investigation game. Zach possessed the names of the other two alleged suicides. Jess possessed nothing. Not a single scrap of evidence.

She'd like to say she trusted the man, but the truth was that he wasn't exactly objective in his goals. He'd made it clear he intended to take down New Horizon, while Jess wanted the truth. Whatever that truth might be.

She extended her hand and wiggled her fingers, wanting to know exactly what Zach knew. "I'll put the addresses in my bag. I can navigate."

Now it was Zach's turn to frown. Surprise filled her when his frown morphed into a slightly crooked grin.

"I never write things down." He tapped one finger to his temple. "It's all right here." A single brow lifted. "Don't you trust me?"

Jess fought the urge to roll her eyes. "Oh, for Pete's sake." She reached into her bag and dug out a pen, pulling a clean napkin from the metal holder. "Tell me before you forget."

He sat back against the bench seat of the booth, crossing his arms over his chest. The sparkle of amusement in his dark eyes left Jess momentarily breathless, she was so surprised to see the glimmer of life there.

"I won't forget." He spoke slowly and surely. "I've got a photographic memory."

This time Jess rolled her eyes before she could catch herself. "You probably have a better memory than most, but there's no reason to risk forgetting that information."

The light of amusement in his eyes faded and he leaned forward. He rattled off two addresses, one just outside town and the other a good forty-five-minute drive away.

As Jessica tucked the napkin safely into her bag, she realized she wasn't sure if having the addresses down on paper had been worth losing the momentary light in Zach Thomas's gaze. She had rather liked having a glimpse of the happy man she'd seen in his photographs.

When his gaze met hers as they slid out of the booth, she was struck by how quickly all signs of warmth had disappeared. When she looked into his eyes this time, the only thing that met her scrutiny was cold.

Stark, blatant cold.

ZACH MENTALLY CHASTISED himself as he followed Jessica toward her condo. She'd pleaded with him to give her time to shower, and he'd caved. The woman had a most unwanted effect on him.

She made him care.

The fear in her eyes was plain to see. Maybe it took a cop to spot the panic crime victims felt after they'd been violated. The intrusion into Jessica's condo was no different, whether any belongings had been taken or not.

Someone had been inside her space.

He'd thought about having her look at mug shots in an effort to identify the man who had approached her on the street, but he hesitated for two reasons.

One, he didn't think the man was a known criminal; more likely he was hired muscle for New Horizon or Whitman Pharma. Those types didn't make the mistake of running into trouble with the law and having their mug shots taken. Those types operated covertly and kept it that way.

The second reason was a bit more personal.

If Zach paraded Jessica down to the station, the guys would figure out exactly what he was up to in a matter of minutes. The last thing he needed was for word to spread he was investigating his brother's death. As far as the department was concerned, that case was closed and forgotten, and they'd been very clear when they'd told him to walk away.

Zach replayed that morning's conversation at the diner, shaking his head. He should have known better than to mention his photographic memory to little miss scientist. Even more importantly, he should have known better than to warm to the woman at all.

The intensity of her mistrust had taken him by surprise. Another sign he was losing his edge.

Of course the woman would mistrust him. Why should she do anything different? He was out to ruin her company and her company's biggest client.

Hell, for all Zach knew, Jessica was cooperating merely to keep information flowing to the powers that be at New Horizon. After all, she was the lead researcher on the HC0815 clinical trial.

The responsibility for any fraud or data tampering would fall squarely on her slender shoulders.

He had a choice to make.

Keep Jessica Parker at arm's length and use her connections only when necessary.

Or keep her so close she'd have no opportunity to work around him.

Experience told him the latter was the choice to make. She was a bright woman. Not only would she be able to help him as the investigation progressed, but as the evidence mounted, she'd be unable to deny New Horizon's wrongdoing.

She was a scientist, after all. Facts were exactly what she needed in order to believe his theory.

Jessica maneuvered her compact car into an open parking space and climbed out. Zach slowed to a stop as she approached his window and leaned against the door.

"There are always spots around the corner." She pointed down the street. "I'll wait right here."

The cool morning air had infused her cheeks with color and her eyes had taken on an alert sparkle.

Yes, he definitely needed to keep Jessica Parker close. At all times.

But as Zach pulled away, stealing a glance in his rearview mirror, his gut caught and twisted. Spending time with Jessica might be the wisest move for the case, but he had a most definite feeling it wouldn't be the wisest move for him.

A SHORT WHILE LATER, as Jess relaxed into the hot spray from her showerhead, she couldn't shake the feeling she'd angered Zach by doubting his ability.

She'd convinced him she needed to freshen up before they paid a visit to the Grant and Kowicki families, so here she stood, spending her entire shower worrying about what the man thought.

Jess had made up the excuse that she hadn't had time to shower the night before, she'd been in such a hurry to get to her parents. She had zero intention of telling him she'd been too frightened to shower in her own condo, even after he'd made sure she was perfectly safe.

Jess shifted her focus from Zach to the information he'd uncovered—the names of the other two trial participants.

She recognized neither from the HC0815 study, so perhaps their suicides and the clinical trial were unrelated. Yet her intuition protested her desire to write off the deaths as random events.

In fact, her intuition screamed that she and Zach were about to discover two more trial participants whose data and adverse reactions—deadly adverse reactions—had simply disappeared from the study case reports.

There had to be a way to uncover exactly what Scott McLaughlin had done. How was it possible that he could code the data to vanish?

She finished her shower, dressing quickly in one of her favorite shirtdresses. She loved the way the seams contoured to her figure, skimming her waist and hips, while still conveying the professionalism she'd worked so hard to achieve.

Jess ran the blow-dryer through her hair, giving her waves a tousle before she twisted the damp strands up into a knot at the base of her skull. A few quick swipes of mascara, moisturizer and creamy lipstick and she was done. In record time, no less.

When she stepped out of her bathroom and into the living area, she found Zach standing in front of her shelves of family photos, his features taut and serious.

Her stomach gave a sharp twist. The sight of the detective studying her family photographs left her unnerved.

"He was diagnosed with multiple sclerosis the day before I graduated from high school." She answered the question she knew he'd ask. The same question everyone asked when they saw or met her father for the first time.

What happened? When did it happen? Did he have an accident? Is he sick?

Sometimes she wished people weren't naturally curious. She wished they'd mind their own business and leave her family alone.

Zach turned to her and frowned. "Actually, I was admiring the size of your trophy." He held up a picture of her in a skimpy majorette outfit, baton in one hand, trophy in the other.

"Oh." Heat fired in her cheeks as she crossed the floor and snatched the frame from his hand. One of his dark brows lifted and she gave a quick shrug. "High school. You know how it is."

Zach's only answer was the slightest hint of a grin at the corners of his mouth.

A second show of humanity in one morning. Would wonders never cease?

Maybe he wasn't entirely dead inside after all.

His smile hinted at the existence of laugh lines, and Jess wondered how long it had been since the man had laughed. Truly laughed.

"What were you talking about?" Zach asked.

Shame filtered through Jessica.

She'd assumed him to be no different than everyone else, when in fact he apparently hadn't batted an eye at the photos of her father in varying stages of physical decline.

"My father," she answered, lifting a framed photo of her parents by her side the day she'd graduated from college.

"Handsome family." Zach turned toward the door. "You should consider yourself lucky. Ready to go?"

Jessica stood rooted to the floor, surprised by his words and tone. Then she realized Zach had no family. Not anymore.

She scanned the frames and the smiles of her mother and father—genuine and loving—and tried to imagine what it had been like for Zach and Jim Thomas to lose their parents so young, so tragically.

Zach was correct—she was lucky.

Very lucky.

He pulled open the front door and stopped to look back at Jess. She quickly returned the frame to its place on the shelf, grabbed her bag and followed him out into the hall.

She'd decided years ago, not long after her father's diagnosis, that her heart didn't have room for anyone but her parents. She couldn't fathom letting another person under her skin, inside the protective walls she'd so carefully locked into place.

Yet, as she watched Zach walk outside, her heart hurt for the man, for the son, for the brother.

Her emotional perimeter had been breached.

Detective Thomas had found his way under her skin, and if she wasn't careful, she might not be able to get him out.

ZACH AND JESSICA didn't exchange a word on the way to the Grant residence. The forty-five-minute drive passed in a less-than-comfortable silence.

Good riddance. He'd begun feeling too comfortable

with the woman, to be honest. No matter. She'd shown her true colors back at her condo.

He'd simply tried to show an interest in her past, and she'd taken his head off over her father's disability. Didn't the woman realize how fortunate she was to have her parents alive?

He drew in a steadying breath, working to keep his anger at bay—the anger fueled not only by Jessica's reaction but also by his reaction to seeing her emerge from the bathroom.

He could try to blame his mood on their conversation, but the reality was that his mood had grown directly out of his frustration with himself.

So much for his theory about his attraction fading away once the woman's buttoned-up persona returned. He blinked, refocusing on the road and the traffic.

Seeing Jessica in her tailored dress with her hair twisted up behind her head hadn't done a thing to erase the fact he was attracted to her. Why now? Why her? She and her work at New Horizon stood for everything he deplored, everything he'd vowed to expose.

The realization did nothing to help his frustration level.

Jessica Parker the woman was a distraction. Jessica Parker the researcher was the only person he needed to focus on. He needed her for her brain and her access to the guts of New Horizon, nothing more.

Zach spotted the turn for the Grant home, signaled, then made the right. He slowed, searching the houses for numbers.

"Right there," Jessica said, breaking the silence. "White Colonial. Blue shutters."

Zach pulled his Karmann Ghia to the curb and cut the engine. "I'll do the talking."

He didn't wait for her response, instead climbing out of the drivers' seat and slamming the door before Jess could do so much as form a sentence.

Out of the corner of his eye, he saw her release the clasp on her seat belt, grab her bag and launch herself from the passenger seat.

"There's no need to treat me like some sidekick."

Zach looked over his shoulder, gaze narrowed. "I'll do the talking."

"I heard you the first time."

Color blazed in her cheeks and satisfaction warmed his belly. He'd let her see the human side of himself one too many times today.

The time had come to remind her of who he was. A detective. A detective out to prove his brother's death had been no accident.

Judging by the look of resignation on her face, she wasn't about to argue. If she was smart, she'd realize he was the trained professional under the circumstances, not her. He hadn't read the course catalogs lately, but he was fairly confident they didn't teach interrogation skills at pharmacy school.

By the time she caught up to him and stepped onto the front step beside him, he'd already pressed the illuminated doorbell. The front door cracked open a moment later, and Zach flipped open his badge, a move he'd made countless times before at countless thresholds. Only this time was different.

This time the case was personal.

Damned personal.

And he wasn't going to let anyone—Jessica Parker included—screw things up.

Chapter Six

"Can I help you?"

Grief painted the features of the woman who answered the door. Zach recognized the look in her red-rimmed eyes, her drawn features and the hollowness in her gaze.

"Mrs. Grant?"

She nodded.

"Detective Zachary Thomas, ma'am. I wonder if you'd have a few moments to talk to us about Amelia."

Surprise flashed in the woman's eyes. "Our daughter committed suicide, Detective. Why would the police be interested?"

"That's what I'd like to talk to you about. We'll only take a few moments of your time."

Mrs. Grant turned her focus to Jessica. Before either woman could speak, Zach made a quick introduction.

"My associate, Jessica Parker."

Jessica gave Mrs. Grant's hand a quick shake. "So sorry for your loss."

With that, Mrs. Grant pulled the front door open and gestured for them to come inside. "I'll put on some coffee."

A few moments later they sat gathered around a well-worn linoleum table—Zach, Jessica, Mrs. Grant and Mr. Grant, who had come in from his yard work at his wife's request.

Mrs. Grant poured four cups of coffee, then sank onto a vacant vinyl chair.

"What's this all about, Detective?" Mr. Grant asked the question before his wife had a chance to settle in her seat.

"First of all," Zach said, choosing his words carefully, "let me say how sorry I am for your loss."

The pair nodded—the tight, polite nod of those in mourning who are quite certain the person offering the sentiment has absolutely no idea how they feel. Though, in this instance, they were wrong.

"My younger brother committed suicide six weeks ago."

Both pairs of eyes widened, obvious surprise painted across their faces.

"He was a sophomore at New Jersey College," Zach continued.

Mr. Grant blinked. Mrs. Grant reached for a box of tissues, then dabbed at the moisture that had gathered at the corners of her eyes.

"I share your grief." Zach hoped the pair wouldn't think him too presumptuous, but he wanted to establish the common bond early on in their conversation.

"Had he been depressed?" Mr. Grant asked.

Mrs. Grant placed her hand over his as if his question was completely out of line.

Zach shook his head and thinned his lips. "Never." He paused for a moment. "His college friends claim his behavior had changed just before his death, but he'd been fine up until then."

"Had something changed?" Mr. Grant asked.

"Harold," Mrs. Grant admonished.

"I'm just asking the same questions everyone asked us after Amelia took all of those pills." Her husband frowned then refocused on Zach.

"She overdosed?" Jessica asked, her voice soft.

Zach gave her a quick glance, noting how sad the corners of her eyes had turned. So the scientist had a heart, as well.

Mr. Grant nodded. "Stole her roommate's painkillers and took them. The entire bottle." He squeezed his eyes shut as he spoke, and Mrs. Grant continued to dab at her tears.

"The roommate had just filled the prescription," he continued. "Coroner said she'd ingested enough to kill three girls her size."

"I'm so sorry," Jessica added.

"Are you a detective, miss?" Mr. Grant asked, his features regaining their focus.

Jessica shook her head and spoke before Zach could answer for her. "I'm a researcher at New Horizon, sir."

At the mention of the name, the Grants sat back against their chairs, faces expressionless.

"Are you familiar with the company?" Zach asked, his heart kicking up a notch in anticipation of their response.

Both nodded.

"Amelia was taking part in a clinical trial." This time it was Mrs. Grant who spoke. "She wanted to be a researcher." Her voice tightened. "Wanted to save lives."

She trained her focus on Jessica. "She was never the same after she took part in that trial. We tried to tell the authorities, but they wouldn't listen."

Zach's heart twisted. He knew the frustration. Knew the assuredness that there had to be another reason for the death other than preexisting depression.

"She developed a temper. Said things that didn't make sense. From what we've learned since her death, she was about to flunk out at Rutgers." Mrs. Grant swallowed down a sob. "She was a beautiful girl. A smart, funny, beautiful girl."

"Which trial?" Zach asked softly.

"HC something," Mr. Grant said. "Supposed to cure Hepatitis C."

"HC0815," Mrs. Grant said in barely more than a whisper.

Zach squeezed his eyes shut and bit back the string of expletives he wanted to let fly.

Jessica visibly flinched as if she'd hoped for a different story—one that didn't implicate her work.

"Did you find any notes about the study in her belongings?" Zach asked, fighting to keep his tone gentle, soothing, when all he really wanted to do was rant and rave at the waste of another young life. "Anything linking your daughter to her work at New Horizon?"

Both parents shook their heads.

"She said she reported to a set location every morning and took her pills." Mrs. Grant had gone pale. "They paid her in cash."

"She had a phone number to call." Mr. Grant squinted as if the entire conversation was beginning to cause him pain. "I think she said it was automated. That's how she reported any side effects."

Zach turned to Jessica, who merely nodded.

"You'd have all that in your records, wouldn't you?" Mr. Grant turned to Jessica.

She gave a slight shake of her head. "Typically yes. But I don't remember seeing a participant file for Amelia. Are you absolutely certain she was a participant?"

Color fired in the father's face. Zach winced.

Jessica had instantly put the man on the defensive with her question.

"I think I know what my daughter was and wasn't involved with." Mr. Grant's voice rose in intensity, and his wife again patted his hand. "Do you want to know what she wanted the money for?"

Zach watched as Jessica nodded, apparently not trusting her voice at that particular moment.

"She wanted it so that she could buy music CDs." He shook his head, then cleared his throat. "CDs. Lot of good they'll do her now."

Zach pulled a business card from the pocket of his

jacket. "I think we've taken up enough of your time." He slid the card across the table and waited for the couple to react.

When Mrs. Grant reached out her hand and pulled the card toward her, Zach continued. "If you find anything or think of anything else about Amelia's work at New Horizon, please call me."

"Is your company to blame for our daughter's death?" Mrs. Grant looked pointedly at Jessica, every trace of weakness gone from her expression.

"I'm not sure. But you have my word that we're going to find out."

A few moments later, Zach and Jessica had settled back into his car. As Zach pulled away from the curb, he could no longer hold back his anger.

"I told you to let me do the talking."

Jessica glared at him, her gaze burning into the side of his face. "I am not a child, Detective Thomas. I am capable of responding to and asking questions."

"Even when you question whether or not their daughter was a participant?"

She fell silent for a long moment. "I could have phrased that question a bit more gently."

"My point exactly."

She pursed her lips. "I apologize, but we still got our information. Their daughter claims to have taken part in the trial, and if she did, someone inside New Horizon has managed to conceal any trace of her participation."

"McLaughlin?" Zach asked.

Jessica shrugged. "Apparently, but at whose direction? Who paid him? And how can we access those records?"

"All good questions." Zach turned to face her as he braked the car for a stoplight. "That's where you come in."

JESS'S STOMACH HAD begun to roll by the time Zach pulled the car to a stop in front of the Kowickis' house, a tidy brick town house not far from the New Jersey College campus.

Part of her wanted to beg her way out of this interview. The grieving faces of Mr. and Mrs. Grant were plastered on the insides of her eyelids, and she wasn't sure she could bear to add additional pained expressions to the vivid image.

Yet she knew she had to hear whatever it was the Kowicki family had to say.

She'd never been one to shy away from the truth, from the facts. She wasn't about to start now. But she wasn't prepared for what they found once Mrs. Kowicki invited them inside.

There, to one side of the living room, sat a veritable shrine. Photographs. Candles. Religious relics. In addition to photos of a younger man Jess assumed to be Roger, there were photos of another older man.

"My husband," Mrs. Kowicki explained. "He committed suicide one year before Roger." She shook her head, looking blank. "You'd think I would have seen the second one coming."

Jess and Zach stood in stunned silence.

"He was never the same after his father died," Mrs. Kowicki continued.

"Was he depressed?" Jess asked, working to keep her tone gentle.

Mrs. Kowicki looked at her as if she were an idiot. "Of course he was depressed." She frowned. "He'd been under treatment since he was a teen."

She blew out a deep sigh. "Inherited it from his father's side of the family." She touched a finger to the boy's photo. "And now they're both gone."

Mrs. Kowicki issued no invitation to sit down and made no offer of coffee or tea. Her message was obvious, at least to Jess. She wanted to be left alone.

"Was Roger involved in a clinical drug trial?" Zach asked, apparently reading the same nonverbal cues Jess had, deciding he'd better get to the meat of their visit before they were asked to leave.

Tears welled in Mrs. Kowicki's eyes and she nodded. "Do you think that had anything to do with what he did?"

"We're not sure, ma'am."

Zach reached out for the woman's arm, but she turned away.

"He drove off a bridge," the woman said flatly. "How could he do that to me? Just like his father. Why?"

"Are they sure it wasn't an accident?" Jess spoke the words slowly, praying she wouldn't add to the woman's blatant pain.

Mrs. Kowicki nodded. "No skid marks. And his

roommate said he'd gone from being distraught to calm. Classic." She shook her head.

"Did he mention anything to you about the drug trial?" Zach asked.

A bitter laugh escaped from Mrs. Kowicki's lips. "He said it was good money. *Good money*," she repeated.

Zach and Jess stood their ground, waiting for the grieving wife and mother to go on.

"He did change after he started taking the pills," she added. "I asked him to stop, but he wouldn't. He brought home the money to me every week. Said he wanted to take care of me."

The woman's voice broke on the last few words, and her shoulders began to heave.

Jess moved without thinking, wrapping her arms around the woman and pulling her into a hug.

Mrs. Kowicki sobbed openly, her body trembling.

Jessica held on tight, whispering soothing words, but when she looked up at Zach, expecting to find concern plastered across his face, she found something altogether different.

Anger. Stark, raving anger.

And based on the daggers shooting from his dark gaze, the emotion was meant for her and no one else.

"HOW COULD A KID LIKE that take part in the trial?"

Zach's anger reverberated loud and clear in his tone. He couldn't care less. He'd held back until he and Jess were in the car and moving away from the Kowicki home.

His heart hurt for the woman, plain and simple. And chances were, if Roger Kowicki hadn't been accepted into the drug trial, he might still be alive today.

Jess stared out the passenger window, her brow furrowed, obviously shaken by what had just happened.

"I don't know," she answered softly, flatly. "I just don't know."

"He had a family history of suicide and he'd been under treatment for depression."

Zach's pulse pounded in his ears. He knew his outburst went beyond Roger Kowicki to the anger he'd kept pent up ever since Jim died. He wasn't being fair to Jess by unloading on her, but right now he didn't care. "What kind of screening do you run over there?"

"Every participant fills out a medical questionnaire." She turned to face him, her features tense. "We trust applicants to give us honest medical histories."

Zach couldn't believe his ears. "You don't do any fact-checking?"

Jess shook her head. "They sign a disclaimer attesting to the fact they're telling the truth."

"Maybe you'd better learn to be more skeptical."

"Why would someone lie like that?"

Zach knew exactly why. Hell, it was the reason that drove most decisions people made every day.

"Money," he said flatly.

Jess squeezed her eyes shut, then reached out to touch his arm. She withdrew her hand quickly, but not before Zach's stomach tightened in response to the gesture.

"You're not going to like what I have to say." Her eyes widened.

Zach kept his focus trained on the road but nodded. "Shoot."

"If Roger Kowicki had a preexisting mental illness, there's no way to put the blame for his suicide on HC0815."

Zach blinked. Was the woman insane? "His mother said his behavior changed."

"Yes, but maybe it changed because his disease was worsening."

"Maybe his disease was worsening because of the HC0815."

"You're not being rational." Jess's tone had turned impatient.

"And you're being nothing but." Zach's anger had moved beyond the boiling point, and he pulled the car to the side of the road, throwing it into Park the second they rolled to a stop.

He turned to face Jess, whose eyes had gone wide. "We're not talking about data, Ms. Parker. We're talking about people. People who have died and people who have lost someone they love."

"I can't possibly begin to understand how you feel," Jess said, "but I know you'd want the truth to come out. What if the truth is that the suicides would have happened with or without HC0815?"

He nodded, working to slow his breathing before he responded.

When he spoke, he did so slowly, enunciating every syllable clearly and distinctly. "How dare you insinuate my brother would have committed suicide if he hadn't been part of that trial."

Jess flinched.

"Are you that unfeeling that you'd write off lives in order to keep that trial going?" he asked.

"This drug has the potential to save millions of lives." Jess's pale gaze searched his face. "We have to be fair about how we approach this."

Zach blew out an exasperated breath. "I'm through being fair. That drug took the lives of my brother, Amelia Grant and Roger Kowicki." He ticked off the names on his fingers. "Who's to say there haven't been more? Who's to say—"

"There weren't other deaths that looked like something other than suicide," Jess interrupted him. "Like Roger Kowicki's might have been."

Surprise tangled with the anger tumbling through Zach. "I thought you were ready to declare HC0815 pure and innocent?"

"I'm trying to be objective, Detective Thomas." Jess sat back against her seat, turning away from Zach, her voice going flat. "No matter what you might think."

Zach cranked the ignition, checked oncoming traffic and pulled the car back out onto the roadway. The sooner he dropped Jessica back at her condo, the better. He planned to hit the ME's records and hit them hard, looking for any area college student's death that might be a misclassified suicide.

Jessica might be wavering on her view of HC0815 and its role in the recent deaths, but he wasn't.

Now all he had to do was continue to build the case, then put the puzzle pieces into place.

Lynn Layton Estep

Hard bottom, he was noticing through... it all; they might be a trampoline, half-sunk...

Kissy-chase he wouldn't, on his own it little time and his tone in the resophonia, could from... Dien pit, and so comes conflict. Frankly uneasy [and] one-sharp, no-solution panic.

Chapter Seven

Jessica worked late that evening, trying to break through the database's layers of protection. She'd fabricated a story about a doctor's appointment to explain taking the entire morning off and then waited for the majority of the staff to head for home before she began digging into the system.

Kowicki's preexisting mental illness had planted a huge seed of doubt in Jess's mind. What if Jim Thomas and Amelia Grant had had preexisting conditions, as well? Perhaps HC0815 didn't cause depression and psychosis but rather exacerbated the conditions where they already existed.

That fact would still negate Whitman's claim that the drug was free of mental side effects, but surely that had to be better than causing the conditions in otherwise healthy individuals.

She'd been hard at work for almost an hour, trying to break through the system's walls, when she received a warning that her user ID was about to be locked out of the system.

Damn.

Without McLaughlin, how would she ever undo whatever it was he'd done? Her problem went beyond simply unlocking the code that randomized participants and assigned numbers instead of names. She had to figure out just what McLaughlin had changed on the case reports—and how he'd done so.

Jess stepped away from the keyboard, knowing better than to leave a permanent record of her snooping—if she hadn't already.

If someone knew where to look, they'd no doubt be able to tell exactly where she'd been—or had tried to be—within the system.

She hesitated momentarily, wondering just how far she should dig, just how deeply she should jeopardize her position and her work. Then she forced herself to take a deep breath and think clearly.

She'd need help from someone more experienced with the system in order to access the information. Otherwise she'd get nowhere.

Jess hadn't planned to take Zach Thomas's concerns to Miles Van Cleef. Not yet. The man was passionate about New Horizon. Passionate about the importance of clinical testing.

The last thing she wanted to do was upset him needlessly and jeopardize the HC0815 trial if, in fact, the suicides could be attributed to something else. Like preexisting depression.

But why were there no intake records for any of the

three victims? She'd checked again, going over the hard copies just in case she'd missed a pertinent document the first time through.

She'd come up empty-handed.

The fact all three forms were missing was more than grounds for suspicion, it was downright alarming.

If Jess didn't know better, she'd swear someone had tried to make the suicide victims' participation disappear. But if the victims had used the automated system to answer study questions, there would be no way to eliminate those answers from the system.

A crosscheck of participant numbers and names would reveal their answers or reveal if their answers had somehow been blocked from the ongoing study results.

Of course, the master access code that would allow her to reveal names and numbers was not one she had. Scott McLaughlin had possessed that key, but that responsibility hadn't been passed on to her.

When she'd taken over as lead researcher, the database management had been handed to David Hansen, an expert in utilizing the New Horizon system.

Hansen had left for the day hours earlier. She'd have to wait, but with any luck at all, he'd be able to give her the answers she needed.

Jess logged out of the system, then logged back in, wanting to make a clean start. This time she inputted her own access code after her user ID to clear the second layer of security, knowing full well her code provided only limited access.

While that access didn't include actual participant identities, it did unlock their demographic data. Age. Sex. Location. Nationality.

Jess flipped from profile to profile, looking for any sort of pattern. At first there seemed to be nothing. A random sampling of college students from area campuses. Freehold. Rutgers. Bergen County. NJC. Another NJC. And another.

Jess frowned, hitting the next-record button repeatedly, disbelieving what she was seeing. Sorted by date, the profiles had changed in one very significant way in the days following the Grant suicide. Without exception, every trial participant had been recruited from the same school.

New Jersey College.

Jess sat back against the seat of her chair and drew in a deep, slow breath.

The intake process had been complete by the time she'd taken over as lead on the trial, and when she'd flipped through this section of the database previously, the fact that a disproportionate number of students were from NJC had escaped her notice.

Did it matter that all participants in almost three months had been drawn from one school? Scientifically, probably not.

The student population at NJC was no doubt as demographically representative as the mix of schools put together, but Jess didn't like the development regardless.

Recruiting the participants from a single source left the door wide-open for tampering and manipulation.

Jess's intuition kicked into gear, screaming that manipulation was exactly what had happened. The fact the change had been instituted immediately following the Grant death smacked of impropriety—and control.

Detective Thomas would have a field day with this information, and rightly so.

She thought again about Van Cleef and telling him what she'd found. Maybe she'd pick up the phone and call him at home.

Jess shook her head. No sense. Plus, did she really know how secure the lab phones were?

She rubbed her eyes and laughed.

Detective Thomas's conspiracy theories were rubbing off.

As if anyone would record company phone conversations.

She decided to wait until morning, just the same. She'd get into work early. That way she'd be able to speak with Miles privately, before most of the other staff arrived.

If her suspicions about the recruitment location were correct, someone behind the scenes had tried to manipulate the controls for the study. And if they'd tampered with the controls and parameters, it wasn't a big leap to the next level of manipulation.

The outcome…and FDA approval.

"I FOUND TWO THAT COULD go either way," the voice on the other end of the line said a split second after Zach answered his phone. "Both at New Jersey College."

Zach recognized the voice instantly. Rick had worked his magic once again.

"That was quick."

"Hey, you go to the best, you get the best."

As much as Zach enjoyed their usual banter, tonight he was in no mood. Much as he hated to admit it, Jess's talk of preexisting conditions had left a seed of doubt in his own mind.

She was right—they had to consider the evidence and circumstances from every angle. They had to leave no stone unturned.

What if Jim really had been depressed and the drug had intensified the condition? What if Zach had failed to see the signs of mental illness in his own brother? Failed to see the symptoms?

Could the deaths be coincidences?

Was it possible?

No.

Zach shook his head. His gut knew he was right— and his gut had never let him down, not in all his years of police work.

"What have you got?" he asked, cutting off Rick's diatribe about research skills midsentence.

"Tracey Remington. Female. Twenty-one. Killed instantly when her car hit a tree during a storm."

"Questionable?"

"Apparently they felt it was a cut-and-dried accident, but you never know."

Rick rattled off the girl's address, then continued.

"The second is a male. Nineteen. Mark Benton. Heroin overdose."

"The bad stuff?" Zach asked, referring to fentanyl-laced heroin that had caused numerous deaths in the region.

"According to the tox screen."

"Why give me this one?"

"There's a little item in the crime beat reporter's notes I thought you'd like."

Zach waited impatiently, wishing Rick would cut to the chase.

"The kid's roommate mentioned he'd been taking part in a drug trial," Rick continued. "Also said Benton had never tried heroin before, at least not that the roommate had known about, but he'd been out of his mind lately and wanted something to numb the pain. That's a direct quote."

A drug trial. Zach's brain locked on to the words and anticipation sprang to life inside him.

"What drug trial? Did the roommate know?"

"Yeah. The kid left his instruction sheet for participation pinned to his bulletin board."

Zach held his breath, wanting so badly to hear the name HC0815.

"Hepatitis C drug," Rick said. "HC0815."

"Son of a—"

"Knew you'd like that." Rick's tone intensified as he rattled off the Benton address. "Go get 'em, buddy. And make sure you call me when this baby's about to break. I'm expecting a front-page exclusive."

Zach stared at the phone for several moments after he'd hung up, stunned by what Levenson had found. He wouldn't know anything concrete until he interviewed the families, but it appeared, at least in Benton's case, that the evidence had just shifted.

And certainly not in New Horizon's favor.

JESSICA COULDN'T SHAKE the sensation of being watched as she walked the short block from where she'd parked her car to her building's front door.

She knew she was being irrational, more than likely letting the past few days get the better of her imagination.

She wasn't sure she'd ever shake the trepidation her encounter with the mystery man had left her with the day she'd first met Zach.

Jess quickly punched in the building's entry code, then closed the door behind her, glancing down the hall before heading to her condo.

Once inside, she threw on both dead bolts, thought about dragging a chair across the door for added security, but talked herself out of it.

She was inside.

The dead bolts were on.

She was safe.

Zach had explained that whoever broke in had no doubt picked the main lock. Once the dead bolts were in place from the inside, no one was getting in.

She kicked off her shoes and headed for the kitchen, settling on cheese, crackers and grapes for dinner.

She headed back toward her bed, glancing longingly at the shower. There was nothing she loved more to help her unwind at the end of a long day, and heaven knew today had been a marathon.

Jess unbuttoned her dress, then tossed it into the hamper, walking boldly toward the shower.

She refused to be intimidated by demons she'd created in her own mind. She was safe inside her condo and she wanted the shower.

The time had come to reclaim the space inside her home as her own.

Jess cranked on the spigot, waiting until the temperature warmed perfectly before switching the flow to the shower setting.

She let her panties and bra drop to the floor where she stood and stepped beneath the spray, pulling the curtain tight behind her.

Jess leaned against the shower wall, fingers splayed against the slick tile, water pulsating off her face and chest. She squeezed her eyes shut and tried to forget about New Horizon—about HC0815—just for a few minutes.

It was no use.

The possibility that negative data had been manipulated haunted her. She'd chosen research and testing as a career because of people like her father. People who deserved a cure—a safe cure.

She couldn't fathom anyone jeopardizing the validity of clinical trials by falsifying or hiding information.

Why would anyone do such a thing? Money? Wasn't that what Scott had said? He did it for the money?

She shook her head.

Innocent lives lost for what? Money in someone's pocket? Ultimate gain by the pharmaceutical company?

Try as she might, Jess couldn't deny something else. New Horizon wasn't the only topic haunting her mind. Zach Thomas had infiltrated her thoughts, as well.

She couldn't get a clear read on the man. One minute he was sullen and grieving, the next he showed a hint of softness and the next he was gruff and authoritative. She arched her brows as she pictured his many moods. No one would ever call the man boring.

There was one constant throughout all of Zach's moods, though. When push came to shove, Jess had no doubt the man would protect her if need be. He hadn't come right out and said as much, but she could read the signs. If she wasn't mistaken, he'd slept in his car outside her parents' house last night.

She smiled. Maybe he wasn't so unfeeling after all.

An unfamiliar noise registered in the midst of her thoughts, and Jess pulled away from the spray of water, straining to hear out into her condo.

Silence.

Fingers of fear danced across her neck and shoulders, but she shoved the sensation away, scrubbing a hand over her eyes.

Her imagination was a dangerous thing. Maybe tonight she'd take a break from her usual bedtime reading and choose something light and fluffy. She frowned. Did she even own anything light and fluffy?

When the noise sounded a second time, a lump knotted in Jess's throat. She wasn't imagining things, and the noise was not one of the regular creaks and groans the old building emitted.

Jess flattened her back against the shower wall and tried to make sense of the thoughts suddenly flooding her mind.

Was there an intruder? Had she remembered all the locks? How could she get to a phone without being seen? Was there time to block the bathroom door, and why had she never put a lock on the damned thing?

Her heart pounded in her ears and her head spun.

If she turned off the water, anyone inside the condo would suspect they'd been heard. Maybe that was a good thing. Maybe they'd leave. But if she left the water running, they'd think they'd succeeded in being undetected. Perhaps she'd be able to sneak past them and somehow get help.

Jess reached up to the rings holding the shower curtain and eased them across the metal bar one by one, as quietly as possible.

Droplets of water hit the side of the tub, splashing onto the tile floor. For once in her life, Jess didn't care about the ramifications. She wasn't concerned about neatness or order. She was only concerned about getting the hell out of her apartment in one piece and calling the police.

Zach hadn't wanted the cops involved in their investigation, but an intruder was another matter altogether.

She reached for the nightshirt she kept hanging on the back of the bathroom door and slipped it over her damp hair, grimacing as the soft cotton clung to her wet body.

Jess pressed an ear to the bathroom door, her hand on the doorknob.

She heard nothing now. Nothing but the spray of the shower and the panicked beat of her heart. She stood still, frozen to the spot for what seemed like minutes—but was no doubt only seconds—measuring her options.

There were none.

There was no way out except through the bathroom door, and she wasn't about to stand there and wait for whoever was in her apartment to come to her.

Jess turned the knob, ducking low so that she'd be out of the immediate line of sight. She listened as she eased the door open.

Still nothing.

Fear clutched at her throat and she sent up a silent prayer.

She scanned the open design of her condo, looking for any movement or shape out of place, but saw nothing.

Then she spotted it. Out of the corner of her eye. The organza sheers that hung at her living room window blew gently in the breeze. The breeze from the apparently open window.

Without another thought, Jess took off in an all-out

sprint, headed straight for her front door. She looked to neither side, keeping her eyes solely on the prize—her escape from the condo and whoever had opened that window.

Jess cursed the dead bolts but threw them off swiftly, jerking the door open and bursting into the hall. When a dark figure moved outside the security door, she screamed, unable to hold back the utter panic that had seized her every nerve and muscle.

"Jess!" A deep male voice shouted. "Jess!"

As she flung herself at her neighbor's door, fists pounding, the voice registered in her brain.

Zach.

She stopped, turning to face the exterior door.

Zach stood at the glass, frantically trying to work the security code, still calling out her name.

Jess covered the space in a sprint, opening the door and launching herself at Zach. It wasn't until he bundled her into his arms and ran a hand over her wet hair that she realized how badly she'd been trembling.

ZACH HAD DRIVEN TO Jessica's condo on a whim, wanting to make sure she was all right before he turned in for the night. As angry as he'd been with her, he'd been unable to get her out of his mind.

He'd spotted her condo lights still on when he parked and had decided to tell her about the questionable student deaths Rick had isolated.

He hadn't been prepared for the sight of Jess, eyes

wide with fear, barreling out of her apartment, dripping wet and definitely scared half to death.

"In there." She breathed the words against his chest. "Through the window. While I was in the shower."

Anger and a fierce protectiveness crashed through him, and he pressed her against the wall next to her neighbor's door.

Judging from the fact no one inside the unit had responded to the commotion, he imagined they were either out for the evening or apathetic. Either way, tucking Jess safely inside was not going to be an option.

"Don't move." He forced calm into his voice, looking intently into Jess's frightened eyes. "You're all right, and I'm sure whoever came in through your window is long gone. There's no way they'd hang around once they knew you'd spotted them."

He spoke the words even though he didn't fully believe them. Sure, whoever had been inside would be long gone now. But had they been gone when Jess had bolted from the apartment? Or had they been hiding somewhere inside, waiting for just the right opportunity to deliver another threat—or worse?

He used his cell to call the department, then searched Jess's apartment inch by inch, careful not to leave any prints. After assuring the intruder wasn't on the inside, he walked to where two framed photos lay shattered on the floor.

One was of Jessica's parents.

The other of Jessica and her father.

Raw fury momentarily blinded him. If whoever did this thought they could get away with terrorizing Jessica, they were dead wrong. When he found out who had done this—and he would find out—he'd make them pay.

For now, he needed to comfort Jessica and reassure her she was safe. If he had to take her back to his house to do that, he would.

He'd automatically assumed Jessica's threats and the investigation were linked, but what if he was wrong? What if she was involved in something else? Zach had never even thought to ask, another sure sign he was losing his investigative edge. He'd remedy that once the police had cleared out.

As if on cue, sirens approached outside, the lights of the cruisers flashing through the condo's windows like strobe lights.

He hurried into the hall, taking Jessica by the hand as he reached for the front door. Her slender fingers felt cool and smooth inside his. He studied her face, far too pale, and dropped her hand.

He shrugged out of his leather jacket, anchoring it around her shoulders, then pulling her close, wrapping his arms around her waist. She stiffened, then relaxed into him, pressing her face into his neck.

The contact sent a jolt through his system—a jolt he wanted no part of.

Zach bolstered his resolve and thought about what he had to do next. He had no choice.

Much as he didn't want to add to Jessica's stress, he

had to caution her about what she said to the responding officers. He wasn't ready to go public with their investigation. Not yet. They needed to keep a lid on their suspicions until they had enough evidence to move quickly and surely.

He pressed his lips to her hair and whispered. "Don't mention New Horizon. Just act as if you have no idea why someone would do this."

She pulled away from him, pale eyes narrowed in disbelief.

"Trust me," he added before she could say a single word.

A split second later the officers were inside, creating mild chaos.

Zach stepped back, hoping Jessica would honor his request and trying not to think about how fast all hell would break loose, not to mention how fast the department would suspend him, if she told the truth.

Chapter Eight

"Why don't you go get dressed."

Zach's words registered in Jessica's blank expression, and she glanced down at her outfit: her nightshirt and his leather jacket.

The police had come and gone, finding no prints whatsoever on the window or the broken picture frames. The absence of prints only meant one thing—the surfaces had been wiped clean.

Princeton hadn't seen rain in weeks, so the ground outside Jessica's window had yielded no footprints.

The officers were at a loss for lack of clues.

Zach, not so much. As far as he was concerned, Jessica's unwanted guest was most likely the same man who had stopped her on the street.

Their previous contact had shown him to be slick and practiced. The methods used tonight fit that same MO. Even the investigating officers agreed the window lock had been popped by a pro.

When questioned about why someone would want to

break into her home and leave the threat, Jessica had feigned ignorance, just as Zach had asked.

While Jessica and Zach had suspicions about New Horizon and the HC0815 study, they had no proof. If word leaked now, the guilty parties would no doubt destroy any remaining evidence.

Reality settled over Zach, leaving him chilled. Someone already knew exactly what they were doing.

Based on the threats Jessica had received and McLaughlin's death, any remaining evidence might already be gone. The possibility existed they'd never uncover the truth.

He squeezed his eyes shut and raked a hand across his face.

He wasn't prepared to accept failure. Not yet.

Jessica reappeared from the bedroom wearing a pair of sweatpants, slippers and a hooded sweatshirt. She'd tucked her curly hair behind her ears, otherwise leaving it long and loose. The casual look became her. Matter of fact, she looked downright beautiful.

Zach ignored the twist his gut gave. "This look becomes you."

"Which one?" Jessica forced a weak smile, dropped her gaze to her outfit, then refocused on Zach. "Sloppy? Or scared spitless?"

He shook his head. "Casual."

Her lips parted, revealing a full smile, something she'd rarely shown him. "Don't get used to it."

The thing was, he could.

He refocused on her intruder, asking the question that had plagued him since the police first arrived.

"Is there any other reason someone might be threatening you?"

Her blond brows snapped together.

"Other than our digging into the drug trial?" he continued.

Jessica's smile slipped, fading completely. "I'm surprised by that question."

Zach gave a quick shrug. "Someone recently reminded me to keep an open mind, consider things from all angles." He forced a smile, hoping to defuse the tension painted across her features.

She shook her head. "We're always worried about competitors stealing our clients' information or compromising their studies, but I can't imagine that would have anything to do with this."

Surprise edged through Zach's system. "I hadn't pictured drug companies to be so cutthroat."

A bitter laugh escaped from Jessica's lips. "Are you kidding? We're talking about billions of dollars here."

Zach sat quietly for a moment, mulling over what she'd said. "So it's fair to say you might be a target for intimidation simply because you're the lead researcher on what could be the biggest medical breakthrough in years?"

Jessica's pale eyes widened as if she hadn't quite thought about the possibility previously. "I suppose so." She shook her head ever so slightly. "But I can't imagine it." She studied him intently, her stare making his insides squirm. "What would someone hope to gain by threatening me?"

Zach thinned his lips. "Maybe they're hoping to gain your cooperation, just as they secured McLaughlin's."

She frowned deeply. "But that would mean a competitor is behind any manipulation of the trial, not Whitman or New Horizon."

Zach nodded, silently admitting the possibility existed he'd been wrong about the guilty party. "Could be."

"So another company might sabotage the trial by hiding adverse reactions." Jessica wrapped her arms around herself. "Once the drug hit market and people developed psychological side effects, that drug would be ruined, if not the company."

"Twisted," Zach answered.

Her gaze narrowed. "But possible."

Zach forced a grin. "I'm still sticking with my theory, but we do need to keep this angle in mind." He pushed to his feet, crossing to where she stood. "You were right about looking at our investigation from all sides."

A wayward strand of hair had escaped from behind Jessica's ear, and Zach reached out to tuck it back into place.

She visibly swallowed, and he let his hand drop to her shoulder for a split second before he lowered his arm back to his side.

He moved to change the subject, to break the suddenly palpable tension between them. "Do you have any beer? Wine? A drink might be a good idea right about now."

Jessica shook her head. "Sorry. Strongest thing here is hot chocolate. Can I fix you a mug?"

Zach laughed softly. "No, thanks. Never touch the stuff."

He followed her to the kitchen, leaning against the counter, watching as she worked, thinking about how soft her hair had felt beneath his touch.

"I found something interesting today in the files."

Jessica spoke the words without looking up from the stove, but the shift in her tone was evident.

"Such as?" He straightened.

She turned to face him, staring intently, a bit of color returning to her cheeks. "Such as every HC0815 participant in almost three months has been recruited from New Jersey College."

"Is that odd?"

She nodded. "Very. It's probably still a representative sampling, but we typically recruit from all of the local campuses."

Zach waited, knowing from her expression she had more to say.

"The change in recruitment happened quite suddenly." She lifted the steaming kettle from the stove and filled her mug. "The day after Amelia Grant committed suicide."

A month before Jim had died.

Zach's mind raced. Had his brother been recruited as part of an effort to control the study? Could this be the first bit of concrete evidence they had?

"Coincidence?" He studied her intently.

Jessica wrinkled her nose. "I've never been a big fan of coincidence, have you?"

Zach shook his head. "And I'm not about to start now."

"So what do we do next?" Determination edged out the fear in Jessica's eyes. "They can't scare me off."

Zach paced a tight pattern beside the counter. "I know you replaced McLaughlin as lead researcher, so why don't you have the same access he had?"

Jessica squeezed her eyes shut and blew out a sigh. "My expertise is in study design, not computers. Van Cleef turned that responsibility over to a man named David Hansen. The candidate I beat out for the promotion."

"Do you think you can convince him to get you deep inside that system without telling him why?"

She squinted as if she were trying to formulate a plan. "I can try."

Zach nodded slowly, his mind running through the necessary steps for them to take. "You take care of that, and I'll chase down the other two possible suicides."

Jessica's brow furrowed and she stepped close. "What are you talking about?"

Damn. Zach had been so thrown by the evening's events he'd forgotten the reason he'd stopped by in the first place.

"I tracked down two other deaths. Both college students. Both causes of death determined to be something other than suicide, but the details are such that the causes of death might be wrong."

He filled her in on the information Rick had given her.

When he finished, she frowned. "I'd have to say it's a long shot."

"Still worth pursuing."

She shrugged. "You're right."

Jessica sank onto one of the stools next to the counter and yawned, pushing the steaming mug away.

"Your adrenaline's fading." Zach moved to her side, pressing a palm to her shoulder.

She didn't move away from his touch but rather placed her hand over his. "I'm glad you were here tonight. I don't know what I would have done without you."

Her words took him by surprise, igniting an unwanted heat deep inside him. He dropped his hand and took a backward step. "You'd have been fine."

Zach glanced around the open design of the condo, then turned his attention back to Jessica. "Are you going to be all right here tonight?"

When she didn't answer, he read the uncertainty in her eyes and, knowing she wasn't the type to ask, offered, "Why don't I sleep on your sofa? Just for tonight."

She swallowed. "I'd hate to impose."

Zach shook his head. "Not a problem. Toss me a pillow and a blanket and you'll never even know I'm here."

A soft smile pulled one corner of Jessica's mouth,

and Zach was struck again by how beautiful she was, just as he was struck by the fact she had no idea of the effect she had on him.

"I'll be right back."

Zach watched as she crossed to a large closet, pulled open the door and reached for a pillow and blanket from inside. She placed the pillow at one end of the sofa, then carefully spread the blanket, tucking the far side into the cushions.

The tenderness of her actions took Zach wholly by surprise. The woman before him was a far cry from the stubborn scientist he'd approached the day of the New Horizon media showcase.

"Zach?"

Her voice interrupted his thoughts, and Zach drew in a slow breath. "Sorry?"

She smiled. "I said your bed's ready, that's all. Is there anything else you need?"

Was there?

Zach was suddenly struck by the thought he needed Jessica herself. He'd focused on the dead for so long—first his parents and now Jim—maybe it was time to focus on the living.

He'd long ago promised himself no more personal involvements, no more pain, and his thoughts about Jessica stunned him. But he couldn't deny they were real.

"I'm fine, thanks." He shook his head, the move in direct opposition to how he felt.

Jessica moved to where he stood, staring into his

eyes for an awkward beat before she threw her arms around his neck and hugged him.

Zach swallowed down his attraction, returning her gesture with a quick hug before taking a backward step. "What was that for?"

"For being here for me tonight. Thank you." She turned and was across the room, pulling a privacy screen between the living and sleeping areas, before Zach could form a response.

"You're welcome," he muttered under his breath.

Thoughts of Jessica battled inside Zach's brain with thoughts of the investigation. Since Jim's death, he'd been focused on nothing but exposing New Horizon and Whitman Pharma. He'd never imagined the person he'd enlist to help him would throw him an emotional curveball he'd never seen coming.

Reality hit and Zach gave himself a mental slap.

Jessica was one of *them*.

She represented the faceless pharmaceutical and testing company executives that had killed Jim with their focus on data—adverse reactions, numbers, outcomes—not people.

His gut protested the thought, and his mind flashed back on the way Jessica had comforted Mrs. Kowicki.

Maybe Jessica really wasn't like the others. Who knew? He sure didn't.

Hell, he just plain didn't know the woman. That's what it boiled down to.

As he settled on Jessica's couch, giving the pillow

beneath his head a sound punch, he decided it was best if things stayed that way.

Once his investigation was over, he'd never see Jessica Parker again. He'd go back to work and he'd go back to his life.

Alone.

JESSICA TOSSED AND turned, unable to sleep. Even though she knew Zach was only a few yards away, asleep on her sofa, she couldn't shake the images of the evening.

The curtains suspended in the breeze from the open window—the window through which someone had entered her home. Her space.

She fought to swallow down the knot of fear in her throat, still present even now. As she relived every moment in her head, she became aware of the quickening of her heartbeat, pounding faster and faster.

Breathe. She had to calm down and breathe.

She flashed on the noise of the frames breaking. The sound of her shower water running. The raw fear she'd felt as she'd cracked open the bathroom door. Her utter panic as she'd fled.

Her total relief at seeing Zach.

Jess squeezed her eyes shut.

She had to be careful. She was growing increasingly reliant on the man—on his presence, on his thoughts, on the sound of his voice.

For someone who was supposedly an objective scientist, she wasn't being very careful about keeping herself from becoming personally involved with the man.

Jessica's heart hurt, her conflicted emotions swirling inside her.

As much as she wanted to help Zach vindicate his brother's memory and find a reason other than the young man's own depression for his death, she had to admit there was still a part of her that wanted HC0815 to emerge untainted.

The pieces of the puzzle certainly pointed to wrong-doing within the trial, but what if there were a logical explanation for everything?

She'd be able to salvage the trial and the pending FDA approval, helping to bring to market a drug that would save millions of lives.

Jess blew out a dejected sigh, knowing there was no way for HC0815 to win this battle.

Whether or not she had proof of the suicide victims' involvement in the trial, the study had to be stopped. Once word of a stoppage leaked to the media, HC0815 would forever carry a mark of uncertainty. That was the cold, hard truth.

But if there was any chance the surviving family members were telling the truth—and why wouldn't they be?—she had to assume the worst.

The drug study was to blame for the loss of three young lives, maybe more.

Jess pulled her comforter tightly around her and tried

to hunker down, tried to escape the tangle of thoughts and theories and faces swirling through her mind.

It was no use.

The questions remained. The faces remained. The images sharp and clear.

One mental image stood out above all else. The photo of Zach with his family. His smile. The bright light in his eyes.

As unobjective as it sounded, Jess had to admit she'd like to have more than a glimpse of that man once the investigation was over. That happy, carefree man.

She knew the thought was irrational and emotional—both things she'd always worked not to be. She laughed bitterly to herself.

Apparently everything she'd been working for at New Horizon might be a sham.

Why should her personal life be any different?

Chapter Nine

An hour into the drive to the Remington house, Zach found himself fighting to keep his mind focused on the goal of his visit and not on Jessica.

She'd emerged from her sleeping area at the same moment he'd woken up on the sofa. Color had fired in her face just as quickly as heat had fired in his belly at the sight of her sleepy expression and tousled hair.

Perhaps he wasn't the only one growing a bit uncomfortable at working—and sleeping—in such close proximity.

He'd stayed at the condo until Jessica was ready to go to work, drinking three mugs of the coffee she'd brewed and picking at the granola cereal she'd fixed for him.

He'd hit a drive-thru bagel shop five minutes after he'd left her condo. It was no wonder the woman was tightly wound, based on how she lived and ate.

The glint of fear had returned to her eyes by the time she'd finished showering and dressing.

Zach couldn't blame her.

This latest threat had left him more than a bit concerned. Not only had the intruder found a way in through the window while Jess was in the shower, but he'd attacked two very personal items. Photos of the people who probably meant more to her than anything in the world—her parents.

Zach knew what it felt like to lose both parents and he'd do whatever it took to make sure Jessica didn't experience that same tragic loss, even if that meant continuing the investigation without her.

As much as he hated the idea of losing her connection to the inside and the New Horizon database, the thought of Jessica and her family being in danger because of his need for answers was a thought he couldn't stand.

Maybe the time had come to remove Jessica from the equation.

Zach was in the middle of his internal argument when he spotted the sign for Cherry Hill, New Jersey. His exit for the Remington residence.

Ten minutes later, he'd successfully found the address Rick had given him and sat parked in front of the split-level home.

A silver SUV sat in the driveway, and the home appeared to be in immaculate condition, though the garden, on closer inspection, showed definite signs of recent neglect.

Zach's chest grew heavy.

He hated dredging up the Remingtons' pain, but this

interview was necessary. If Tracey Remington had been a participant in the Whitman Pharma trial, there was a definite possibility her accident hadn't been an accident at all.

Zach stepped up to the front door and pressed his finger to the bell, drawing in a deep breath while he waited for a response.

The yapping of a small dog grew closer and closer, as did a woman's voice.

"Just a minute, please."

Zach pulled his badge from his pocket, wanting to put Mrs. Remington at ease the moment she opened the door.

The door snapped open, and the woman frowned as if his unfamiliar face had been a surprise, as if she'd been expecting someone else.

"Detective Thomas, Princeton Borough. I wonder if I could speak to you for a few moments. It's about your daughter."

"Tracey?" The woman's features went instantly slack. "I don't understand."

"There have been a handful of deaths among area college students, and I'm following up on each of them." Zach grasped for a reason that would gain the woman's trust without giving away his investigation. The fewer people who knew he was out to get Whitman and New Horizon, the better. "I understand your daughter was involved in a traffic accident."

She nodded, gesturing for Zach to cross the threshold. "Please, come in. Can I get you something to drink?"

"No, ma'am." Zach stepped into the tile foyer, instantly struck by the immaculate interior, decorated as though a design magazine was due any moment for a photo shoot. "I won't take but a few minutes of your time."

Mrs. Remington led him into a formal living room. As he sat on a pristine white sofa, the source of the yapping became apparent. A tiny fur ball scooted from beneath the sofa and launched itself at the woman's lap as she settled into a wingback chair.

"What can I help you with, Detective?"

"First of all—" Zach leaned forward, hands clasped, doing his best to convey his sincerity "—I'm terribly sorry for your loss."

She gave him a thin-lipped smile, but unlike his visit to the Grants, this time Zach offered no information about Jim. He wanted to keep the focus solely on Tracey Remington.

"I was wondering if your daughter's behavior had changed in any way during the days or weeks before her death."

The girl's mother frowned. "I'm not sure I know what you mean, Detective."

"Was she angrier, quieter, louder, depressed?" He narrowed his gaze, waiting for her reply. "Anything of that nature."

"She was a young woman who had just been dumped by her boyfriend," Mrs. Remington answered. "I'd have to say she was all of the above."

"And the night of the accident. Where was she headed?"

Mrs. Remington blew out a sigh, visibly unhappy about having to revisit the circumstances of her daughter's accident. Zach could hardly blame her.

"She was headed back to campus. She'd been here for the weekend, but she had to get back. She had exams the next day."

Zach nodded. "And she simply lost control?"

"It seems that way. The investigators thought she might have swerved to avoid hitting an animal, based on how sharply she veered off the road."

Zach dreaded his next question, knowing it would do nothing but plant a seed of doubt and regret in Mrs. Remington's mind. But it had to be asked.

"Mrs. Remington?"

She nodded, eyes wide.

"The deaths I'm following up on, they were all suicides."

The woman shrunk back into the depths of the chair.

"Could there be any possibility—"

"No." Her one word interruption was spoken sharply, as if the question had been asked and answered previously. "She was upset about her boyfriend, but she would have never taken her own life. She was passionate about living, Detective. Tracey would never have chosen to die." She shook her head, sending her blond bob swinging. "Absolutely not."

It was obvious Zach wasn't going to get anywhere with that particular tactic.

"Have you ever heard of a company named Whitman Pharma, Mrs. Remington?"

She nodded, looking at him as if he had two heads. "Everyone has, Detective. They're one of the giants in this state."

Zach unclasped his hands, moving to stand. He gestured toward the front door. "I'd best be on my way. Thanks for your time."

She frowned. "Was that all you wanted to ask me about Tracey?"

Zach nodded. "I told you it wouldn't take long."

Her next words stopped Zach cold.

"Tracey was so excited to be working on that Whitman Pharma study. She wanted to be a researcher, you know. Wanted to help people."

Zach dropped his hand from the doorknob and turned to face Mrs. Remington. Her features had brightened, as if remembering her daughter's dreams had somehow brought her back.

She smiled. "See? She'd never kill herself. She wanted to save people, not see them die."

"Do you remember the name of the study, Mrs. Remington? Did she have any paperwork that you know of?"

The woman shook her head, her forehead crumpling. "Something with numbers. She mentioned it once."

Zach pulled a card from his pocket and pressed it to Mrs. Remington's palm. "If you remember or if you find anything, give me a call. Please." He added the nicety out of respect for the woman's environment.

She was obviously used to both manners and the finer things in life.

She made a clucking noise with her tongue. "I wish I could remember that name for you." She gave her head another shake. "Tracey was so proud of that study. She wanted so badly to make a difference." Her dark eyes widened. "Her cousin died from Hep C, you know."

Zach did his best to keep his features expressionless. "Did the study involve a drug for Hepatitis C?"

Mrs. Remington nodded. "I just can't seem to pull the name out of my brain. Sorry I wasn't more help."

Zach fought the urge to hug the woman. "You've been more helpful than you know."

And she had been.

As he pulled away from the curb, he mentally added a piece to the puzzle and savored the sense of satisfaction sliding through his veins.

The authorities might have classified Tracey Remington's fatal crash as an accident, but if the girl had been involved with HC0815, there was no doubt in Zach's mind the drug was the true culprit, not a tricky turn in the road.

Jessica had to find a way to match the names to participant numbers. She had to. They needed concrete proof in order to make a move.

He revisited his earlier thought about booting her off the investigation. Guilt and determination tangled inside him.

Truth was, he needed her. Needed her more than he wanted to admit.

There was only one solution to the problem. Zach would have to do whatever it took to keep Jessica Parker safe, even if that meant sleeping on her couch night after night until their investigation was complete.

But what would they do if she wasn't able to match the names and numbers? There had to be another way to corroborate the families' stories about the students' participation in the trial.

What was it Jessica had said? A disproportionate number of the participants came from New Jersey College.

He'd worked a case once where the school psychologist there had been instrumental. A real resource. They'd worked together several times over the past few years, and she'd left three messages for him since Jim's death.

Maybe now was the perfect time to return her call.

JESS RUBBED A HAND across her tired eyes as she sat at her desk. She hadn't slept a wink and she couldn't say for sure if her insomnia had been caused by the break-in or by the tension of knowing Zach was in her condo.

She'd walked into the New Horizon building realizing she didn't remember the drive to work. Sure, the route had become routine, but the reality was she'd been so focused on thoughts of Zach and HC0815 and threats to her parents that she hadn't been paying attention.

She needed to be more careful.

Now more than ever.

She needed to talk to Hansen, and as much as she dreaded asking the man for anything, she might as well get on with it.

As she made her way down the hall toward his work area, Jess couldn't help but study every fellow employee she passed. Who was behind the threats? Someone inside New Horizon? Someone from Whitman? Someone from a competitor?

And why?

To shut her up? To get her to stop digging into the current trial's adverse reactions? Or to get her help?

She drew in a steadying breath as she approached Hansen's door. She needed to compose herself, needed to shove all errant thoughts from her mind.

She had to focus.

Jess had never considered David Hansen to be a warm and fuzzy person. Of course, most of the scientific types at New Horizon were anything but warm and fuzzy, Jess included. Yet Hansen had carried a chip on his shoulder since she'd been promoted to lead researcher on the Whitman study.

Van Cleef had told her in confidence Hansen felt he deserved the position, even though his background was in computers, not research.

Jess had done her best to include the man in major decisions and in planning, but his attitude had made it more and more difficult to work with him, let alone like him.

In every trial, the computer randomized participant numbers, creating an anonymous list of subjects who used an automated system to phone in their status and any adverse reactions they were experiencing.

Only one person within New Horizon had the ability to break the code, so to speak, if it ever became necessary to pull a particular individual's responses or data.

Up until a few weeks ago, that person had been Scott McLaughlin.

That person was now David Hansen.

Jess stood at the door to the computer area where Hansen sat hunched over a set of printouts. She drew in a deep breath and silently told herself what she was about to do was necessary. She and Zach needed to unlock that code, and Hansen was the only person with the ability to help them.

Much as she hated to be a suck-up, there was no time like the present to polish her skills.

"How are the new responsibilities going, David?" Jess breezed through the door, hoping Hansen hadn't seen her standing just on the other side. "Can't think of anyone more deserving."

Hansen never took his eyes from the screen. "Smooth as silk. Nice job at the media showcase, by the way." He reached up, running a slender hand through his too-long dirty-blond waves. "Didn't see you on the tour afterward." He glanced up at her then, his pale green eyes piercing, belying the polite tone of his voice. "Get a better offer?"

Jess stood her ground, keeping her forced smile plastered on her face. "Not at all. One member of the media needed a bit of special attention, that's all." She waved a hand dismissively. "A few pointed questions about HC0815."

David nodded, then refocused on the screen. "If you're done with the chitchat, I've got some major inputting to do."

Jess brightened, moving to stand behind him. David hit a key that made the screen automatically switch to a swirling New Horizon logo.

"I can't work with you standing over my shoulder." The annoyance in his tone was palpable.

Jess stepped to one side, tilting her chin. "My apologies. I didn't realize you were so particular about your work space."

Hansen lowered his chin until there was no way Jess could get his attention without stooping to his level, which was something she had no intention of doing.

"I wondered if you could help me with an anonymous tip we received?"

That got his attention. He lifted his gaze to hers, squinting. "I'm surprised you'd want my help."

Jess shook her head. "Why wouldn't I? The caller said they had firsthand knowledge of a participant who had fabricated study responses." The ease with which she made up the story amazed Jess. "I was hoping you'd help me match the name to a participant number so that we could pull the data from the mix."

Hansen frowned. "Why would I do that?"

"Because it makes sense." Irritation began to simmer

in her belly. If she had her way, Hansen and his holier-than-thou attitude would have been long gone the day she took over the trial. But hirings and firings were Van Cleef's realm, not hers.

"Only makes sense if you believe the caller," he answered. "Plus, the system is programmed to isolate discrepancies. Did you tell Van Cleef?"

Jess shook her head again. "I didn't think this would be such an issue."

She spoke the words, but her mind locked on something Hansen had said.

The system is programmed to isolate discrepancies.

He was right. The software program had a built-in failsafe for anyone phoning in bogus information. Would it also work to help someone in the know isolate reactions as serious as psychosis?

Of course it would.

"You'd better talk to Van Cleef." Hansen swiveled his chair to provide Jess with a view of his back and nothing else. "I can't do anything without a directive from the top."

"I am the top." Jess did her best to hide her growing frustration with the man's attitude, but based on her tone, she wasn't doing a very good job. "The top of this study."

His only response was a shrug of his shoulders. "When it comes to the system, I answer to Van Cleef. No one else."

Jess stepped back into the hall without wasting another moment with the man.

She had a new plan. A new approach. She'd generate a discrepancy report.

They were typically only run at the end of the trial, but there was no reason not to check the information early. She gave herself a mental slap. She should have thought of this sooner. Much sooner.

Even if McLaughlin had somehow coded the adverse reactions to show as something else, surely she'd be able to spot a pattern, wouldn't she? Unless he'd coded them to appear not as adverse reactions at all.

Her heart sank. She knew instantly the report would do her no good.

McLaughlin had been nothing short of brilliant. If he'd covered up information, he wouldn't have left the possibility of something as simple as a discrepancy report exposing him.

She had to try nonetheless.

Short of talking to Van Cleef, she was out of options.

Marcie Stone was a force to be reckoned with. Zach could see it in the way students greeted her as they made their way down the walkway through campus.

With more salt than pepper in her close-cropped hair, she wore the knowing smile of a survivor, of a person who had seen much in her life and lived to talk about it.

Zach had liked her from the moment they'd met two years earlier. The woman had an uncanny way of knowing what drove people to do what they did, and her expertise had helped him narrow down the profile of more than one suspect.

The October air was crisp yet mild as they made

their way through campus, walking at a leisurely pace, weaving in and out of groups of students either on their way to class or on breaks between sessions.

"And how about you?" Marcie said, breaking the silence as they made a wide arc around an impromptu soccer game on the lawn. "How are you handling your brother's death?"

The abrupt question startled Zach, though it probably shouldn't. Marcie was one of the most perceptive people he'd ever met. And one of the most blunt.

"Life goes on," he answered. "What other choice is there?"

"You can seek revenge." She stopped, staring at him pointedly. "Though typically nothing good ever comes of that."

So she'd already assumed he'd come to talk about New Horizon and their role on campus. Smart lady.

"What if it stops what happened to Jim from happening to another kid?" He widened his gaze, tipping his chin toward a pair of students deep in conversation. "If someone was knowingly exposing them to a danger, wouldn't you do whatever you could to stop that person?"

Marcie nodded, letting out a soft sigh. "There is that, and that's a natural response, but revenge alone won't fix your heart."

"It would certainly be a good start." Zach released a bitter laugh.

Marcie stopped, pinning him with a solemn stare. "The only thing that's going to fix your heart is forgiveness."

Zach couldn't believe his ears. "Forgiveness? They killed my brother. I'll never forgive them."

She smiled softly, then shook her head. "You need to forgive Jim. For dying. He didn't do it to hurt you."

The psychologist's words sucked the air from Zach's lungs as if she'd pulled a plug. He had never blamed Jim, had he?

Zach frowned and Marcie patted his arm. "Just think about it," she said. "I think you'll surprise yourself when you take a deep look inside."

That was just it, Zach thought. He'd spent a long time avoiding deep looks inside. He had no plans to start now.

"Listen." He raked a hand through his hair. "I know you've got a busy schedule, and while I appreciate your concern, why don't we get to the real reason I'm here."

"New Horizon?" Her smile brightened.

Zach nodded. "Any extra visits to your office from kids taking part in their trials?"

Marcie waggled a finger at him. "You know full well I couldn't tell you if there were."

He arched a brow. "But are there? Have there been?"

The psychologist tipped her head back, glancing up at the crystal clear autumn sky. "Let me just say that, based on gossip around campus, if certain students had sought help when they started experiencing unfamiliar emotions and paranoia, perhaps I could have intervened in time to help them. Maybe I would have been able to put my finger on whatever had caused the change."

Zach straightened. "So you're saying their depressive behavior was new? Not preexisting?"

"I'm saying it's always frustrating for someone in my field to feel as though they might have helped if only they'd been given the chance."

Marcie's words haunted Zach as he headed back toward home. He'd decided against a visit to the Benton home, knowing in his gut the kid had taken part in the trial. The instruction sheet in his apartment said it all.

His visit to Marcie had left his mind spinning, and he wanted to get back to his notes. Back to the pieces of the puzzle.

They might have helped if only they'd been given the chance.

Zach knew what she meant—knew what she was trying to say without coming right out and saying it.

The depressive episodes had been new. Sudden.

Zach also knew how she felt.

He liked to think he might have been able to help Jim if only his brother had given him the chance.

Now he'd never know.

And that was the toughest part of his grief to swallow.

JESS HAD SPENT THE bulk of the afternoon utilizing excuses to stay in Hansen's lab, doing whatever she could to watch over his shoulder as he worked. He'd switched to routine profile inputting, no doubt wise to her efforts to catch a glimpse of the inside of the system.

He'd been gone for two hours now—the entire staff had been gone for two hours—and here she sat, doing her best to gain access to the database. A hacker, she wasn't.

She'd inputted the commands for the discrepancy report and now had only to wait for the system to spit out the data. In the meantime, what could it hurt to give accessing the guts of the database another try?

Zach had phoned to tell her about his meeting with Mrs. Remington. Jess had found no record of Tracey Remington's participation in the study. She'd run Benton's name, as well, also coming up with nothing.

The system beeped, announcing the production of the discrepancy report. Her heart sank lower and lower into her belly as she flipped through page after page of results.

The only discrepancies reported were mild. Upset stomachs. Headaches. Dizziness.

Nothing close to suicide. Nothing close to a mental complaint at all.

If she didn't know better, Jess would think the report had been cleaned up.

Her pulse quickened. Matter of fact, she was sure of it.

Angered by the results and stymied by her continued inability to unlock participant identities, Jess decided to pull the application archives one more time.

She hadn't checked them since she first looked for Jim Thomas's paperwork, and while she didn't expect to find a paper trail for the other four names, she might uncover something that would make a difference—something that would snap another piece of the puzzle into focus.

She pulled the file folders for the last five months of applications and began flipping through them one by one, application by application, searching for five names.

Jim Thomas.

Amelia Grant.

Roger Kowicki.

Tracey Remington.

Mark Benton.

Jess worked in reverse order, expecting any of the suicide victims who might be there to be in the more recent files. It wasn't until she reached the last folder, the files from five months earlier, that she found one of the names.

The name that had started the entire investigation.

Jim Thomas.

Jess held her breath as she scanned the information, her heart beating faster. She hadn't found Jim's application in her preliminary search and she was certain she'd pulled this folder.

Hadn't she?

She traced her finger down the sheet, stopping at the box used by New Horizon's intake manager—the final determination whether or not to allow an applicant into the study.

The status of Jim Thomas's application sucked the air out of Jess's lungs.

Rejected.

Had Zach's brother never been part of the study? Or had someone planted a phony application?

Jess slipped the single sheet from the stack and neatly

folded it in half and then in half again. She tucked it into the pocket of her lab coat and returned the folders to the file cabinet, using caution to place them exactly as they had been before she'd removed them.

An acrid smell tickled her nose and she winced.

What on earth—

Before she had another moment to think, the hard-wired smoke detectors began to screech, one after the other, deafening in their intensity.

Smoke.

Fire.

Jess reached for the phone just as the lights went out, plunging the lab into darkness. Going by memory, she fumbled until she found the receiver, then pulled it to her ear.

Dead silence.

The phones had gone out with the power.

The smell of smoke grew stronger, and fear sparked to life in Jess's belly. She had to get out. Now.

But she'd left the discrepancy report on the other side of the lab.

Jess knew the alarm would trigger an automatic response from the local fire department, but based on how quickly the smoke was finding its way into the lab, the source of the blaze must be close.

There was no time to spare.

She fumbled in the darkness, feeling her way by running her hands across the front of computer stations and work desks. She did her best to judge how far across the room she'd been working and on which desk she'd left the report.

Fear squeezed at her throat.

How on earth had a fire started? And how had it spread so quickly?

Her fingers bumped up against the stack of papers and she breathed a sigh of relief.

She plucked the report from the desk just as something brushed against the back of her lab coat. She spun, blinded by the darkness, raising one arm instinctively, defensively.

Something crashed over her, sending her to the floor and the report flying from her hand.

Jess struggled to pull herself to her knees, struggled to move, but she found herself pinned.

Pinned beneath what felt like someone's foot.

Before she could scream for help or fight to defend herself, pain exploded at the side of her head.

As the pressure on her back disappeared, and the stench of smoke and burning material grew heavier and thicker, Jess's conscious thought began to fade.

She willed herself to move, to get up, to crawl away, but she couldn't.

Her body wouldn't respond.

The last sound she heard was the sound of sirens in the distance.

Far in the distance.

Then Jess heard nothing.

Nothing at all.

Chapter Ten

Zach's cell phone rang as he sat in front of Jessica's building, waiting for her to come home from New Horizon. She'd said she planned to work late, but this was getting ridiculous.

He glanced at his watch. Nine o'clock. He hoped her lateness was a sign she'd hit the mother lode of information.

Zach frowned when he spotted the incoming number in the ID window.

Rick Levenson.

Had he found more HC0815 victims?

"Hey," Zach barked into the phone. "Out of doughnuts already?"

"No, man." Rick had dropped his voice low, and the urgency in his tone sent the hairs at the base of Zach's skull bristling to attention. "You'll never believe what just came over the scanner."

"What?"

"Three-alarm at New Horizon."

Jessica.

Zach's heart lodged in his throat. "Injuries?"

"Too soon for reports. Just thought you'd like to know."

"Jessica was going to work late."

The curse Rick muttered beneath his breath was impossible to miss. "You'd better get a move on then."

A split second later Zach had done just that, cranking on the ignition and peeling out into the roadway without a glance in either direction.

He raced across town, rolling through yellow lights and pushing his luck on a few reds. He flipped on the local twenty-four-hour news station, but apparently news of the fire hadn't made it over the wires yet.

He mentally berated himself. He never should have let Jessica go into work. Hadn't he told himself he wasn't going to let her out of his sight?

Yet if she didn't keep up appearances at New Horizon, they'd never have a shot at breaking this thing wide-open.

As he made the turn into the industrial park that housed the clinical trial management company, the lights of countless emergency vehicles lit the night sky.

Zach's throat tightened and nervous energy set his every nerve ending on edge.

If anything had happened to her...he'd never forgive himself. He would have let her down just as he'd let Jim down.

Zach pulled the Karmann Ghia to the side of the

drive, stopping short of the action, knowing he'd never get any closer unless he was on foot.

A crowd of people from a twenty-four-hour printing company had gathered along the sidewalk, and Zach stepped close to a young lady standing by herself.

"Any word on injuries?" he asked.

She nodded. "They brought one person out." She pointed toward an emergency medical team's van. "Over there." The young woman shrugged. "I'm not sure how bad, but whoever it was wasn't walking."

Zach's chest squeezed. "How about the fire?"

"Someone said it was well-contained to begin with. Weird, though, isn't it?"

"Weird," Zach repeated as he hurried away, headed straight for the EMTs.

A uniformed cop tried to block his way, but Zach pulled his badge, flashing it as he nodded to where someone sat huddled in a blanket.

Was that blond hair? Could it be?

"My fiancée," he lied, "she was working late."

The officer waved him past. "Lucky the fire crew got here when they did. She might not have made it otherwise."

"Thanks."

Zach fought to swallow down the lump in his throat as he took off in a jog toward where the lone victim sat deep in conversation with an emergency worker.

When she tipped up her chin, gesturing toward the New Horizon building, her profile became clear.

The curve of her jaw.

Her nose.

The way she continually tucked her hair behind her ears.

Jessica.

Zach sagged with relief but immediately bolstered himself, racing to her side.

Jessica turned toward him as he approached, scrambling to her feet. Moisture welled in her eyes. "You're here."

He bundled her into his arms, pulling her tight against him, his hands splayed on the small of her back. When she tucked her face into his neck, his body responded—stomach tightening, pulse quickening.

"I shouldn't have let you come here."

"It's my job." Her breath brushed against his collar.

The relief flooding through him took his breath away, as did the depth of emotion the thought of losing her had inspired.

He suddenly had an amazing thought. Keeping Jessica safe had become more important than proving New Horizon wrong. He'd realized it on the drive over.

Beating New Horizon and Whitman meant nothing if anything happened to Jessica.

"Are you okay?"

"She needs to take it easy," the paramedic answered. "Took quite a bang on the head and some smoke inhalation."

"I'm okay," she said softly.

"You fell?" Zach asked.

She pulled away from him slightly, giving the slightest shake of her head. "Someone hit me."

Zach's relief gave way to anger—hot, rolling anger. "Hit you?"

She nodded. "Whoever it was got away. The firemen didn't see anyone but me." Her expression turned intense. "They're not going to get away with this."

Zach pushed her out to arm's length and stared into her frightened yet determined eyes. Even injured and obviously rattled, the woman had a light inside her like nothing he'd ever seen before.

"It might be time for you to take a break from all of this."

"No way." Jessica's gaze searched his face, then narrowed. "Are *you* all right?"

Zach lowered his mouth to hers, the contact abrupt yet strong. Her lips parted beneath his, and he kissed her deeply, though only for a moment. When he broke away, he tightened his grip on her waist.

"I am now," he answered.

A look of utter amazement and surprise had replaced the determination he'd seen in her eyes a moment before. She no doubt hadn't thought him capable of such a blatant and public show of emotion.

Neither had he.

"How badly are you hurt?" he asked, amazed by the concern and protectiveness flowing through his veins.

Jessica reached up to rub the side of her head. "Just a big bump. I'll be fine."

"Were you hit before or after the fire broke out?"

"After."

"Did you get a look at him?"

She shook her head. "It was pitch-black, and whoever it was came at me from behind." Jess squeezed her eyes shut as if trying to erase the memory of what had happened. "We've probably lost most of the files. I was in the archive room."

"Let's get you home," he said, gently shifting one arm fully around her waist as he turned to look for the officer in charge. "Have they already questioned you?"

Jess nodded, pulling the blanket more tightly around her shoulders.

"Cold?"

Another nod. "Freezing all of a sudden."

Zach pressed a kiss to her temple. "Your nerves probably just kicked in. It happens once the adrenaline wears off."

"You'd think I'd be getting used to it," she said flatly.

Zach tightened his grip on her and caught the eye of a buddy from the force, motioning the officer over.

"What are you doing here, Thomas?" The man's features tensed. "Thought you were on leave."

Zach tipped his head toward Jessica. "Friend of the family."

"That so?" The officer's mouth pulled into a crooked grin.

"She all done here?" Zach asked.

The officer nodded. "We'll call you if we need anything else, Ms. Parker."

Jessica swallowed, forcing a smile. "Thank you."

"How bad is it?" Zach nodded toward the building just as a pair of firemen headed back inside.

"Limited to one office and work area," the officer answered. "Looks pretty deliberate. Destroyed several file cabinets."

Jessica visibly winced, a pained expression on her face.

The young police officer patted her arm. "You must have a guardian angel."

Jessica nodded her agreement as Zach turned her away from the building.

Looks pretty deliberate.

Zach weighed the officer's statement as he bundled Jessica into the passenger seat.

Someone hit me.

Jessica's words sent a cold shudder slicing through him.

Whoever had set the fire had not only meant to destroy evidence but they'd also meant to destroy Jessica.

But who? And how would they get inside the security-protected building?

The fire and the attack had to be inside jobs.

Maybe the time had come for Zach to take his suspicions and what little evidence they had to the station, suspension or no suspension.

Jessica's safety was worth more than any damned job.

One thing was certain. From now on, he had to keep Jessica under his watchful eye at every moment.

Zach gave himself a mental shake. There was one more thing he needed to do, and she wasn't going to like it.

The time had come to wrap her up in cotton and hide her away. He had to boot Jessica off the case.

Whether she agreed with him or not.

JESSICA RODE IN SILENCE, staring out into the night sky as she clutched an ice pack to her head.

She had no doubt what the official investigation into the fire would show. Arson. Corporate sabotage.

Groundbreaking drugs were big business—billion-dollar business. Was that enough motivation for someone to set the fire? Possibly. But Jess knew better.

Her intuition screamed that she and Zach were getting too close for someone's comfort, much as she didn't like to rely on intuition.

But who?

"We'll be there in just a minute." Zach's words sliced through her thoughts. "Anything I should stop and get for you?"

"No." The fatigue in Jess's voice surprised her. "I just don't want to go to my condo tonight."

"I wouldn't have let you if you had."

Protectiveness rang heavy in Zach's words. For once in her life, Jess didn't mind. She didn't mind the man taking over, stepping in and being her protector. It felt good, actually.

Right now she was tired and more than a bit over-whelmed. Having Zach by her side not only felt good, it felt right.

She stole a glance at his profile, tracing the line of his jaw with her gaze. He hadn't said a word about his kiss. Neither had she.

Perhaps he was going to act as if it had never happened, but she wasn't sure that was a possibility as far as she was concerned.

As much as her head wanted to tell Zach it could never happen again, her heart completely disagreed. Zach's arrival and his kiss had felt like an anchor, grounding her in the midst of the chaos. She wasn't sure getting emotionally involved with the detective would be a wise move, but the truth was it was already too late to worry about that.

She'd been emotionally involved since she'd met the man. Since she'd seen the pain on his face as he talked about his brother. Since she'd seen the love in his eyes in the photos of his family.

Much as she'd tried to ignore the attraction, the more time she spent with the man, the more he intrigued and challenged her. Whether he knew it or not, Zach Thomas had effectively chipped a huge hole in the emotional barrier she'd worked for years to keep in place.

"I'll come around and get your door."

Zach's voice startled Jess. She hadn't realized they'd already reached his house.

Jess pushed open the passenger door and climbed out

of the small sports car. Her head throbbed with the motion and she winced.

Damn. Just what she didn't have time for. She pulled herself taller, doing her best to hold her features steady.

Worry instantly creased Zach's forehead. He'd seen straight through her efforts. "You all right?"

"Sure." She forced a smile as they walked toward the front door, she, determined to do so without leaning on Zach and he, hovering so close it was a miracle he hadn't tripped her.

"I'll get you something to wear."

Zach left her in the living room as he vanished down the hall. He was back within a minute, towel in hand.

"Bathroom's on the right, and I set out some sweatpants, a few flannel shirts. Take whatever you feel comfortable in."

Jess gratefully took a quick shower, thankful to wash the stench of the fire out of her hair and off her skin. She slipped into a faded pair of navy sweatpants and smiled as she buttoned up a thick flannel shirt.

The amount of comfort she found in wearing Zach's clothes amazed her, and she let the emotion fill her, for once in her life not trying to reason her feelings away.

When she cracked open the bathroom door, Zach stood in the hall, apparently having waited there to make sure she was all right.

He tipped his chin toward the bedroom. "I put a tray in there for you. Some soup. A mug of hot chocolate."

He shrugged. "I was trying to think of what might go down easily."

He held out his arms for the pile of clothes she'd bundled into her arms, and Jess willingly turned them over. "My lab coat's dry-clean-only." She shook her head. "Maybe we should hang it outside or something to get that smell out of your house."

"Not a problem."

A few minutes later they'd settled together in the bedroom, Jess beneath the covers and Zach perched on the side of the bed.

She'd drained the soup, having been far hungrier than she thought she'd be, and now sipped the hot chocolate, waiting for Zach to bring up the inevitable.

"We need to talk about tonight." He visibly drew in a deep breath, then pressed his lips into a thin line. "I should never have kissed you. I apologize. It won't happen again."

Jess would be lying if she tried to tell herself the emotion running through her veins was anything other than regret.

"I was so relieved to see you," he continued. "I guess you could say I was overcome by the moment."

Jess said nothing, dropping her focus to her cup to hide any disappointment that might show in her eyes. What was wrong with her? Rationally she knew stopping anything with Zach before it started was the smart move. The irrational part of her brain, however, protested. Loudly.

"I spoke to an old friend today." He reached for her hand, startling Jess when he interlaced his fingers with hers. "She made me realize I still haven't dealt with Jim's death, and at least in her mind, going after New Horizon and Whitman isn't going to help me do that."

Jess straightened. "You're not giving up, are you?"

He couldn't. They couldn't. They were getting close. She could feel it in every inch of her body.

Zach shook his head. "I'm not. You are."

Anger began to simmer in Jess's belly. Did the man honestly think he could tell her what to do?

She sat back against the headboard, slipping her fingers free of Zach's. "If I stop now, whoever set that fire tonight will think they won."

Zach shrugged. "So let them think that. So what? I'll take what we've found so far and run with it."

"Not without me, you won't." Determination fired in her belly, strong and hot. "I mean it."

He smiled as if she'd sleep on what he'd said and wake up realizing he'd been correct. The man had a lot to learn about women. Especially this one.

She'd never met a problem or question she didn't see through to solution. She wasn't about to start now.

"I ran a discrepancy report tonight just before the fire." Jess took a swallow of hot chocolate, then pulled the quilt a bit tighter around her. Just talking about the fire had sent a chill racing through her.

"We run them for every trial," she continued. "Typically there are always two or three off-the-wall answers submitted by participants. Either they're crackpots or they just want to have fun with us." She paused for a beat, taking a breath, trying to ignore the pounding at the side of her skull.

"We automatically adjust for those answers, and you become fairly adept at spotting them."

"But?" Zach asked, hanging on her every word.

"But there aren't any for HC0815." She studied his expression, the intensity of his gaze having the same startling effect on her now that it had had the day they'd met. "Nothing more than a headache."

She leaned forward, fully focused and sure of what she was about to say. "I think McLaughlin—or someone—programmed the responses to recode themselves. That way, any adverse reactions would either enter the program as mild side effects or no side effects at all."

"Someone could do that?" Amazement glimmered in his dark eyes.

"If they wanted to badly enough." She tucked her still-damp hair behind her ears. "It's not easy, but it can definitely be done."

"Can someone undo it?" He stared at her, slight creases wrinkling the skin around his eyes.

"I didn't have any luck with Hansen today," she explained. "But I'll try again tomorrow. If anyone could do it, he could."

Zach grew silent and Jess knew exactly what he was thinking. But she wasn't about to do as he'd asked. If

HC0815 had been the cause of the suicides, she'd do whatever it took to blow the truth wide-open.

"You can't put me out to pasture yet, Detective Thomas."

Their gazes locked, an undeniable spark passing between them. Jess leaned even closer, uttering her next words in barely more than a whisper.

"You need me."

HOURS LATER, ZACH LAY awake next to Jess. She'd fallen asleep as they'd talked, and he'd been out in the living room ever since.

Until he'd decided to check on her.

He'd crawled onto the bed beside her, intending only to make sure she was fully covered and had her head supported properly.

The truth nipped at the base of his brain.

Oh, who was he kidding?

He reached out to touch a lock of her hair, letting the silky strand slide between his fingers.

The heat that had been simmering all night coiled inside him, winding tighter and tighter. He longed to touch her. Longed to kiss her again. Longed to take her into his arms and make love to her.

Zach squeezed his eyes shut, willing his attraction to Jessica to go away—permanently—but it was no use.

The combination of her stubbornness, her intellect and the fire in her eyes had worn down his resolve to ignore his feelings. The fact that she took his breath away every time he looked at her hadn't helped his case, either.

You need me.

Her words toyed with him, taunting him.

He did need her, but he needed her for more than her connections to New Horizon.

She'd found her way into his heart—a place he'd thought safely shuttered for good.

If he was smart, he'd find a way to get her out.

Fast.

Chapter Eleven

Jess rolled up the clothes she'd worn the day before and shoved them into a trash bag. No amount of washing and drying would ever rid them of the stench of the fire's smoke.

Zach had washed and dried them twice the night before, and she'd already washed them once today since Zach had taken her back to her car then followed her home.

Full of disappointment, she eyed the outfit lovingly. One of her favorites.

Her lab coat was another matter. Was it even worth taking to the dry cleaner's?

She gave a mental shrug.

Nothing ventured, nothing gained.

She'd drop it off on her way into New Horizon. Dr. Van Cleef had called her that morning to check on her condition, and she'd told him she needed to speak with him.

The facility would be running with a reduced staff while a professional crew cleaned the smoke and fire damaged area, but he'd told her he wanted to keep the

HC0815 trial going. They'd come too far to let anything jeopardize the study now.

Jess stepped into her bathroom to check her makeup and reached for her hair, twisting it behind her head as she'd done countless times before.

The move ignited a dull ache where she'd been hit.

She released her grip on her hair, letting the waves fall about her shoulders. Her headache eased instantly.

Jess frowned at herself in the mirror. Her French twist was her signature hairstyle for work, and without it she felt a bit…well, casual. And casual was a look she'd never gone for.

She thrived on control. Neatness. A place for everything and everything in its place.

Jess stared at her reflection.

She supposed there was a first time for everything.

Ten minutes later she'd pulled to the curb in front of the dry cleaner's. She tucked her lab coat into the crook of her arm as she pushed through the shop's door.

She waited patiently as the owner wrote up her slip, then turned to leave. A little voice at the base of her brain was nagging at her, but why? What?

Then she remembered.

"Hang on a second, please." Jess pivoted, retracing her steps to the counter. "I think I left something in the pocket."

The clerk handed back the lab coat, and Jess stuck her hand first in one pocket and then the other.

She was forever making notes to herself and shoving

them into her pockets. But this time the item her fingers fell upon wasn't a note at all.

She pulled the folded sheet from her pocket, the recognition instant.

She'd almost completely forgotten.

Jim Thomas's application.

Rejected.

Jess winced, then returned her lab coat to the counter. She sat for a long moment staring at the paper after she dropped into her driver's seat.

How could she have forgotten to tell Zach about this? Her heart caught. Truth was, she dreaded telling Zach about this.

The man was one hundred percent sure his brother's suicide had been caused by HC0815. How would he ever accept that his brother had never taken part in the trial?

Jess traced a finger over the notation made in the intake box. No initials.

Odd. Certainly not standard operating procedure. And if she wasn't mistaken, the handwriting was not Scott McLaughlin's, the person who would have made the ultimate decision regarding participation.

She refolded the sheet and tucked it into her bag.

No need to breathe a word of this to Zach. Not yet. Not until she got to the bottom of just who it was that had completed the form…and when.

WHEN JESS ARRIVED AT New Horizon, Van Cleef was waiting for her in his office. As she settled into one of the chairs next to his desk, nervousness skittered through her, though she couldn't put her finger on why.

Perhaps she was nervous because Zach had expressly told her not to speak to anyone inside New Horizon until they knew exactly what and who they were dealing with.

But surely Zach hadn't meant Dr. Van Cleef.

She and he were kindred spirits, both having watched disease steal the vitality from someone they loved. They both knew the value of scientific research when conducted carefully. And honestly.

Van Cleef would want to know if someone was sabotaging the HC0815 trial. And he'd help Zach and Jess get to the bottom of the mystery. She had no doubt.

She might not have a copious amount of hard evidence, but she surely had enough to make her boss sit up and take notice. Plus, she had the word of McLaughlin himself. He'd admitted to altering data.

New Horizon was Van Cleef's life. Jess knew he'd do whatever it took to protect the company, even if that meant closing down the most important trial they'd ever conducted.

"The police tell me they suspect corporate sabotage," Dr. Van Cleef said as he sat back in his chair, eyeing Jess. "If only you hadn't been here so late, you might have been spared."

Jess forced a tight smile. "Wrong place, wrong time."

Van Cleef's eyes narrowed. "Why were you here, Jessica?"

She hesitated momentarily, then plunged in, divulging everything she and Zach had uncovered. The additional suicides. The missing applications. The questionable discrepancy report.

He held up a hand to stop her. "But the data to date shows not a single adverse reaction anywhere close to psychosis or suicidal ideation."

"McLaughlin said he'd altered the data somehow to hide the reactions."

Van Cleef squinted at her, scowling. "It's not possible."

"But it is." Jess sat forward in her seat, intent on making Van Cleef believe her. "All anyone would need is the trial's master access key. Once they were inside, they could alter the computerized response codes. Participants would continue to phone in their results through the automated system, but the codes the computer would be programmed to enter would be incorrect."

She climbed to her feet, leaning her palms flat against the cluttered surface of his desk. "It's why the discrepancy report shows nothing out of whack. The discrepancies have all been compensated for."

Van Cleef sat silently for what felt like minutes. He leaned back against his seat and blew out a sigh.

"It can't be done." He spoke the words flatly.

Jess's heart fell. "What do you mean?"

Van Cleef thinned his lips, then spoke. "When we developed the New Horizon system, we made sure such manipulation could not take place. Changes to a study's automated case reports are not possible without an original change and a secondary change. They must come from two different administrators."

He leaned forward. "I am the second administrator, and you can be sure I made no such change."

Jess sank back to her seat, deflated. "But Scott said—"

Van Cleef's eyes softened, showing the compassionate side Jess had grown to love and respect during her employment at New Horizon.

"Scott McLaughlin had a drug problem. The man would say anything for money. Perhaps he thought you'd reward him for saying what you wanted to hear."

"But the accident—"

"Was an accident," Van Cleef interrupted. "For all you know, Scott stepped directly into the van's path."

But he hadn't. If anything, he'd tried to get out of the van's path, only to be plowed down.

"What about the participants?" Jess asked. "Where are their applications?"

His white brows drew together. "Their families all claim they took part?"

Jess nodded.

Van Cleef made a notation on the small notepad he always kept within arm's reach. "The intake files were all destroyed last night."

Disbelief washed through Jess. "I thought the cabinets were fireproof?"

He glared at her, his expression suddenly bordering on angry. "Apparently the pertinent drawer was left open."

Open? There was no way she'd left that drawer open. Absolutely not.

Van Cleef didn't have to express his suspicion. Jess could read it in his eyes. But for the time being, she'd keep her mouth shut.

"What about revealing participant names?"

He looked at her as if she'd committed blasphemy. "And jeopardize the validity of the trial?"

"People are dying, Dr. Van Cleef." Jess forced the words through her throat, now tight with a desperate sense of urgency. "Dying."

"You know what a lawyer would say in a court of law, Jessica?"

She shook her head.

"Hearsay." Van Cleef's gaze narrowed. "It's all hearsay."

Jess could barely believe her ears. "I could see one or two, but five? How can you dismiss five deaths?"

"Five deaths that might have nothing to do with this trial."

"Then reveal the names and disprove me."

Jess knew she was way out of line in challenging the man, but she didn't care. Suddenly her job and her career with New Horizon meant nothing. She wanted no part of a company or an industry that wasn't willing to examine its own behavior at the first sign of mismanagement.

"I'll take it under advisement." He stood, rounding his desk and coming to a stop directly in front of Jess.

"You mustn't breathe a word of this, Jessica. Your suspicions could destroy HC0815 unfairly."

Jessica turned toward the door, suddenly needing to distance herself from the trial, from Van Cleef, from everything. Her stomach roiled sour and she battled down the bile rising in her throat.

What on earth was going on?

Either she and Zach were completely off base or the cover-up was so extensive even Van Cleef had been duped.

Jess headed toward David Hansen's work area, knowing that particular lab had survived the fire unscathed, but when she turned the corner to his office, the chair in front of his computer station sat empty.

She picked up Hansen's phone and dialed the receptionist. "Would you page David Hansen for me, please?"

"Mr. Hansen didn't report for work today."

Suspicion tapped at the base of Jess's brain. "Did he call out?"

"No, ma'am. He just didn't show up."

"Thank you."

Jess hung up the phone and hurried back toward her temporary workspace.

Didn't show up?

Heaven knew she wasn't a David Hansen fan, but she couldn't remember a single day of work the man had missed. Not one.

A jumble of possibilities battled for position in her mind. Theories. Reasons. Suppositions. Next steps.

One thing was clear. She had to get back into Van Cleef's office when he wasn't there. Chances were HC0815's master access key was buried somewhere on top of the man's cluttered desk.

If Hansen was a no-show and Van Cleef wasn't going to help her get the information she needed, she'd simply have to get it herself.

ZACH SAT AT HIS kitchen table and nursed what had to be his fifth cup of coffee. Jessica had insisted on going into New Horizon.

He'd conceded it was important she kept up appearances and showed she wouldn't be intimidated, but that didn't mean he had to like it.

She'd assured him as long as she visited company offices only during working hours, she'd be safe. After all, the place would be swarming with recovery crews trying to repair damage from the fire.

When his cell phone rang, Zach expected the caller to be Jess, but Rick Levenson's number appeared in the window instead. Zach frowned.

Now what?

Levenson didn't wait for a greeting before launching into conversation.

"I thought since you're so hot to trot on New Horizon, you might like to know the final determination regarding former employee Scott McLaughlin's death."

Zach straightened, coming fully alert. His biggest gripe about being out on leave and neck-deep in a covert investigation was the fact he'd been completely removed from all department news and resources.

If not for Rick, he probably would have heard the news about McLaughlin in the paper, just like everyone else.

"Tell me." He squeezed his eyes shut, waiting for whatever it was Rick had to say.

"Apparently your friend Scott owed a lot of money to the Gambone family."

We all have our vices.

Scott's words played across Zach's memory, but a frisson of surprise rifled through him just the same.

"Gambling?" he asked.

Rick made a snapping noise with his mouth. "Drugs. Investigating officers found a nice stash at his home and a message on his cell threatening his life if he didn't pay up. They got a break when they picked up a minor player on another charge. The guy flipped."

"Any arrests yet?"

"No," Rick answered. "But I thought you'd like to know the motive."

Zach blew out an exasperated breath. He thought he had known the motive. Could it be that McLaughlin's death had been completely unrelated to their case?

If the man was buried in debt, Zach supposed manipulating the HC0815 data for quick cash made sense, even to someone committed to scientific truth. But that still left the primary question unanswered.

Who had paid Scott to make the changes?

"When are you going to fill in the blanks for me on

this thing?" Rick asked. "Nothing better than an investigative exclusive to blow things wide-open."

Silence beat across the line as Zach considered Rick's words.

He was right.

Zach had been waiting for the perfect moment to bring in the rest of the force, but what if he took a media approach instead?

The timing would have to be perfect, and he'd need Levenson's sworn promise to keep a lid on things.

"If I remember correctly—" Zach thought back to the many times he'd tipped Levenson that a case was about to break, ensuring the reporter an exclusive "—you owe me, correct?"

"Ri-ight." Levenson drew the word out into two syllables.

"Not over the phone." Zach pushed to his feet, gathering his notes into a pile. "Meet me at Battlefield Park in twenty minutes, but not a word of this leaks until I give the okay, understood?"

"Zach, my friend, you have a deal."

JESSICA'S MIND WAS SO wrapped around the mystery of HC0815 that she found it impossible to give even the appearance of working.

She'd feigned dizziness from her head injury and ostensibly headed for home a bit before noon.

In reality, she'd headed directly for New Jersey College and the man who had once been her mentor.

Terrance Davis. Head of the medical research department.

She'd worked alongside Davis for years and respected the man. Admired his work. Valued his opinion.

But why on earth would he be a party to the Whitman trial using only NJC students? Such a controlled step went against everything Davis had taught her about clinical trial recruitment.

She pulled her car into the parking lot outside the medical research department building and cut the engine. Glancing at her watch as she hurried along the sidewalk, she hoped she wasn't too late to catch the man. Ten after twelve. She might very well be out of luck.

Davis was fanatical about taking a lunch break. Always had been.

Relief whispered through her as she stepped inside the building. Davis's office door sat wide-open. She blinked, working to help her eyes adjust to the dim indoor lighting.

"Professor Davis?" She hesitated at his door, knocking lightly against the jamb.

"Jessica." The man's face brightened instantly and he took off his glasses, straightening from his seat. "To what do I owe this unexpected pleasure?"

"I need your input on something," she answered as they exchanged a quick handshake.

His warm expression morphed to one of concern. "I heard about last night's fire. I trust you're all right?"

Jess gave a tight nod and smiled. "I'm resilient."

Davis emitted a soft chuckle. "You always were." His lips curved into a smile once more. "Now what can I help you with?"

"It's about the Whitman trial." She'd decided to avoid beating around the bush. She and Davis had always been of the same mind-set. Get to the point and get to it quickly.

He leaned a hip against his desk. "I'm listening."

"Almost three months ago, all of the recruitment began to come from your campus exclusively."

Davis's dark brows lifted, then he narrowed his eyes.

There had been a time when Jess had been wowed by the professor's movie-star good looks—dark brown hair, chiseled features, bright blue eyes.

She realized as she looked at him now that he no longer impressed her. Jess had come to favor the looks of a real man. A more rugged man. Someone who had experienced more life—like Zach.

"I believe that was a suggestion made by New Horizon." He nodded his head as if to confirm what he was saying. "It's more convenient for dosing to have the participants all attend the same school."

"But what about providing a good sample?"

"Not a problem." He gave a quick lift and drop of his shoulders. "Anything else?"

"Don't you find it alarming that four of the NJC participants have died—three of them definitely suicides?"

Shock registered in his otherwise controlled features. "Four?"

"And one at Rutgers."

Davis said nothing, moving around to stand behind his desk, as if the physical barrier would block Jess's questions.

"I had no idea."

"That you'd lost four participants?" Jess knew she was leading Davis's response, but she'd do just about anything at this point for an admission.

Just as quickly as the man had looked flustered, calm returned to his features.

His dark brows drew together. "What I meant was that I had no idea we'd lost so many students. As a college." He moved away from his desk, taking a step toward Jess. "Did you know copycat suicides often occur on college campuses after an initial suicide?"

She nodded, the gesture not meant to signal agreement but rather to encourage Davis to finish making his point so that she could resume her questions.

"People commit suicide, Jessica," he continued. "They've been doing so since the beginning of time."

"But these four were all taking part in the Whitman Pharma trial."

His vivid eyes widened, almost as if he'd practiced the surprised expression he now wore. "I have no knowledge of that."

Jess knew this man. She'd worked with him and for him long enough to know when he was lying. And he was definitely lying to her now.

"Fair enough." She shrugged, hoping to convince him she'd bought his story.

"I understand New Horizon recruits solely through our department now, using only NJC students, but their participation is anonymous and I haven't heard a thing about suicides within the trial."

He returned to his chair, sitting down and reaching for the phone, delivering the clear nonverbal cue their meeting was over.

"Jim Thomas." Jess stepped close, leaning her palms against his desk. "Roger Kowicki. Mark Benton. Are you going to tell me you don't know any of these students?"

He shrugged using only his eyes. "Suicide is sometimes the tragic consequence of pressure, Jessica. Maybe these three students were at their breaking point."

"What about Tracey Remington?"

Anger fired in his carefully controlled gaze. "She was one of my best students. A lot like you, actually."

"According to her mother, she was part of the study."

"She drove her car into a tree, Jessica." He narrowed his gaze and looked at the door. "Her death was a horrible shock, but it was an accident. Now if you'll excuse me…"

Jess read him loud and clear, taking a step toward the door. "I appreciate your time, Professor Davis. Let me know if you remember the other three."

"Always happy to see one of my favorite students." He smiled broadly. "I know you'll succeed beautifully over at New Horizon. Just look how devoted to the validity of the study you are."

As Jess made her way out of the building and toward the parking lot, her intuition screamed that Davis had been lying. He had obviously already known about the suicides. Anyone on campus would have. But his claim of ignorance about whether or not they'd been participants in the trial felt forced. Practiced.

What would he have to gain by lying?

Reality hit her like a backhanded slap.

What if he were part of the plot? Part of the cover-up? Part of whoever it was that had manipulated the study?

Of course he'd lie to dissuade her from her suspicions and he'd also assume she'd believe him. After all, he had been her mentor.

The question now was, would he call someone to report Jessica's visit? And if he did, would that someone want to meet?

Jess pulled her cell phone from her bag, punching in the number for Zach's phone as she dropped into her driver's seat.

Terrance Davis appeared on the sidewalk, walking briskly toward the parking lot before she had a chance to hit the send button.

She let the phone fall back into her bag and slid down in her seat, hoping to make herself as close to invisible as possible.

The professor might simply be headed out to lunch. But if, by chance, he was on his way to meet someone tied to the clinical trial, she had to know.

She had to follow him.

When Davis climbed into a late-model Lexus sedan, Jess shoved her car key into the ignition and twisted. Her hybrid's engine purred to life.

Jess waited for Davis to pass behind her, then she eased her car out of the parking space, following the man at a discreet distance.

Not a bad car for a college professor. She couldn't help but wonder how he'd paid for it.

She followed him for no less than ten minutes, disappointment washing through her when he pulled into the parking lot of a popular restaurant.

Damn.

She'd gotten her hopes up for no reason. The man was obviously going out for a meal, nothing more. Between Zach filling her head with conspiracy theories and her own love of suspense, she'd really let her imagination get carried away.

Jess had no sooner decided to drive away then she saw a tall, statuesque blonde emerge from a parked Mercedes. As the woman climbed into the passenger seat of Davis's sedan, Jess got only a brief glimpse of her, but a brief glimpse was all she needed.

After all, she'd seen this particular woman at the New Horizon facility enough to recognize her with absolute certainty.

Blaire Wells.

Vice president of product development for Whitman Pharma.

Now, if she and Terrance Davis were romantically involved, then Princeton was an even smaller world than Jess had previously thought.

But if Blaire Wells and Terrance Davis were involved in some sort of clinical trial cover-up together, the puzzle pieces had just gotten a whole lot more interesting.

Jess sat back against her seat and blew out a deep breath.

How many millions in stock value would Wells personally lose if HC0815 failed to gain FDA approval and go to market?

How forgiving would a woman in Wells's position be of adverse reactions found during the trial period? Would she find them unacceptable? Or would she write them off as necessary risks?

If Blaire Wells had conspired to keep those reactions quiet and enlisted Terrance Davis's help on the recruitment end, she'd committed a huge breach of ethics.

The FDA would want Whitman Pharma's head on a platter.

This time when Jess punched in Zach's phone number, she waited for him to pick up. When he did, she spoke quickly and distinctly.

"What would you say if I told you I'm watching Whitman Pharma's VP for product development cozy up to the head of NJC's medical research department?"

The expletive Zach muttered beneath his breath was unmistakable.

"I'd say. Are they making small talk or grand plans?"

As Jess listened to Zach's question, Wells launched herself from the passenger side of Davis's car, immediately adopting an aggressive fists-on-hips pose. Davis exited his door, then rounded the hood of the car, obviously trying to calm the woman.

Jess narrowed her gaze, studying the pair. "Definitely not small talk, and if I didn't know better, I'd say they were arguing."

Loud but indistinguishable voices filtered through her car window.

"Definitely arguing," she repeated.

"Any idea about what?" Zach's voice rose on the last word, as if he suspected what the answer might be.

"I'm thinking their argument might have something to do with the questions I just asked Davis about the suicides and the clinical participant recruitment at NJC."

"Perhaps a debriefing session is in order." The hopeful tone of Zach's voice brought a smile to Jess's face.

"I thought you'd never ask."

Chapter Twelve

"So he denied knowing the students?" Zach sat down next to Jessica, handing her a bottle of beer even as he took a swig of his own.

"With the exception of Tracey Remington." She pulled her legs up beneath her, curling into the arm of the sofa and tucking the beer against her stomach instead of drinking it.

Zach nodded toward the bottle. "I can get you something else."

She shook her head. "This is fine."

"Hot chocolate, maybe?"

She grinned, the move warming her lovely features. "I meant to ask you just when it was you started stocking hot chocolate?"

Busted. Zach arched his brows. "I used to be a Boy Scout."

"Sure you did." She took a sip of the beer and made a face. "Sorry." She handed the bottle back to Zach.

"One hot chocolate coming up."

Jessica followed him into the kitchen. The work area was small, and while he had always felt cramped whenever someone else was in the kitchen with him, having Jessica by his side inspired no such negative thoughts. In fact, having Jessica by his side felt... right.

"Can we prove he's in bed with Whitman?" she asked.

Zach shot her a sideways glance and grinned.

Color fired in her otherwise pale cheeks. "You know what I mean."

"I do." He filled the teapot and set it on the stove, cranking the flame a bit higher. "My best guess would be financial records, but we're not going to have access to those."

"Why not?"

He leaned back against the counter, crossing his arms while they waited for the water to heat. "We'd need a warrant."

"And for that we'd need an active, police-sanctioned investigation." Jess finished the thought for him.

Zach nodded. "Exactly."

"So we're back to square one." She pressed her lips tightly together.

"Feels like it."

"I'm going into New Horizon tomorrow."

Jess began to pace a tight pattern. Zach watched her brow furrow in concentration. No one could ever accuse the woman of making a decision lightly.

"Van Cleef never works on the weekends," she continued. "His wife's quite ill and he spends his days off by her side."

"I'm sorry to hear that," Zach said.

Jess nodded. "Me, too. She's a terrific lady." She held up a finger. "But it's convenient for us because it will give me the chance to get inside his office and search his desk."

Zach's internal alarm began to chime. "I'm not sure I like the sound of that."

She gave a quick shake of her head, sending her blond waves flying. "It's not what you think. He's an organizational nightmare." She gestured widely. "His files are all over the top of his desk. He likes piles, not filing drawers."

Jess tipped up her chin to meet Zach's gaze, her pale eyes intent yet shimmering with excitement. Zach's stomach tightened.

"He's got the master access key somewhere on that desk." She patted her chest. "And I'm going to find it. If he won't help me, I'll go around him."

Admiration welled inside Zach. Jessica had come a long way from the corporate goody two-shoes toeing the company line he'd met at the media showcase. Had that really been just a few days earlier?

"What's that look for?" She shot him a slight frown.

The kettle whistled, and Zach reached to turn off the flame, thankful for the opportunity to look away as he said his next words. "I was thinking what an incredible person you are."

He poured boiling water on top of the chocolate powder at the bottom of the mug, waiting for Jessica's response. She made none.

Zach lowered the kettle back to the stove, then lifted his gaze to Jessica's. Her expression had gone soft, and warm color had fired in her cheeks.

"You're not so bad yourself," she said.

She reached her hands up through her hair, running her fingers through the strands before she moved to tuck the waves behind her ears. Zach reached for her, covering her fingers with his.

He stroked the length of her hair, then cupped her face in his hands, kissing her before she could protest and before he changed his mind.

But instead of offering a protest, Jessica offered an undeniably welcoming heat.

She laced her fingers behind his head and pulled his mouth firmly over hers. Their tongues tangled, dancing between each other's lips. When a soft groan escaped from her throat, the desire simmering deep in Zach's core exploded.

He skimmed his palms down to her shoulders, dropping them to her waist and pressing her body to his. Her curves fit all of his angles as if they'd been made for each other. He felt himself go hard against her belly, and a soft gasp slipped between her lips, her breath mixing with his.

Zach traced his fingers along the curve of her waist, caressing the swells of her breasts with his thumbs.

Jessica arched her body against his, dropping her kisses to his jaw, then down the length of his neck.

The intensity of his need threatened to overwhelm Zach, and he took a backward step, letting his hands slide back to Jessica's waist. Her mouth gaped open, a look of sheer surprise washing across her flushed features.

"I want you to be sure you know what you're doing." He spoke the words softly, as if he was saying them to himself just as sincerely as he was saying them to Jessica.

A soft smile pulled at one corner of her mouth. "I've never been more sure of anything. You?"

Was he sure?

He was sure he wanted her—wanted her as he'd never wanted another woman. But did he know what he was doing? Really doing? He was opening himself up to emotional need. Emotional desire. Emotional hurt.

He could walk away now, stop what was happening before they went any further. He could play it safe.

But as Zach looked into Jessica's questioning gaze, he knew he didn't want to walk away. For once in his adult life, he didn't want to play it safe.

He wanted Jessica.

The truth was that simple.

He pressed a quick kiss to her lips, and her smile grew wide.

"I'm very sure," he said, taking her hand. He led her through the living room and down the hall toward the bedroom.

Jessica hesitated just outside the door, and he stopped

to look at her, expecting to see doubt in her pale gaze. Instead he saw nothing but desire for him. He'd never seen a sight more beautiful.

Zach closed the space between them, backing her against the wall and splaying his hands to either side of her head. Jessica bit down on her lip and grinned up at him.

He was lost.

He hoisted her into his arms and carried her into the bedroom. As he lowered her onto the bed, he trailed kisses down Jessica's neck, unbuttoning her blouse and tracing his lips along her flushed skin. Zach nipped at the lacy edge of her bra, savoring Jessica's response as she bucked up against him.

She reached to unhook the front clasp of her bra, and Zach captured her hands in his. She stared up at him, her gaze expectant.

"Are you sure you're all right?" he asked. "Your head—"

"Is much better now." Her words flowed over him like a soothing balm.

He released his grip on her hands, and Jess opened her bra, offering herself to him. Zach lowered his mouth into the valley between her breasts and nipped lightly, first at one breast, then the other. He teased one nipple between thumb and forefinger as he closed his mouth over the other.

Jessica's response was instant. She writhed beneath him, moaning softly.

He slid both hands to her waist, pulling her tightly

against him as he suckled each breast, alternating from side to side.

"Zach." The sound of his name on her lips set something inside of him on fire, and the coil of want he'd held under control for days broke free, spreading through him.

He reached for her zipper and lowered the tab, exposing her flat belly and the lacy edge of her panties.

His erection pulsed against his jeans and his head spun.

As if reading his mind, Jessica reached for him, first untucking his T-shirt, then unbuttoning his jeans.

Zach slipped her slacks and panties over her hips and down her legs, then stood, dropping his jeans and boxers to the floor.

Jessica visibly swallowed and he stood still for a moment, taking in the length of her naked body with his gaze.

"You're beautiful."

Jessica shifted on the bed, opening herself to him, but instead of entering her, he lowered his mouth to the inside of her thigh, wrapping his hands around her bottom as he traced his tongue along her tender flesh to the moist heat waiting for him between her legs.

He teased her, nibbling lightly before trailing kisses along the inside of her other thigh up to the side of her shapely knee.

Her breathing had gone shallow, coming now in soft panting breaths.

He retraced his mouth's path, running his lips back down her soft flesh to taste her hot, wet center.

Jessica gasped, moving beneath him. "You're killing me," she murmured.

"We can't have that." He smiled against the folds of her flesh but didn't stop, instead plunging his tongue inside her until her panting turned to gasps. He trailed one hand up over her belly until he brushed the swell of her breast, then teased her nipple once more, working the bead between his thumb and forefinger.

"Zach." His name on Jessica's breath this time was barely more than a whisper.

He nipped at her tender flesh lightly, and her body shuddered, pulsing beneath his touch. As he drove her over the edge of her orgasm, he fought to restrain his own release, wanting nothing more than to be inside her, to feel her heat surrounding him.

Zach waited until her breathing settled a bit, then he traced the curve of her hip, her waist, her breasts with his mouth, tasting every beautiful inch.

He lowered himself between her legs, holding steady as he looked into her hungry eyes, urging her silently to stay with him, to look at him as he made love to her.

She did, instinctively moving with him, opening herself to him as he drove inside her, thrusting to the hilt of his shaft. Her mouth opened and she rolled her neck, but Jessica never took her eyes from his.

Their gazes locked in an erotic dance as their bodies moved together, stroking, caressing, loving each other until Jessica went over the edge of release again, this time crying out loud.

Zach's own release followed just seconds after hers, and as his body shuddered with a surrender he'd never known, he lowered his face to her neck and held on tight, not wanting to let her go.

Not then.

Not ever.

JESS WOKE THE NEXT morning filled with a delicious ache. She rolled toward Zach's side of the bed, only to find the sheets turned back and a dent in the pillow where he'd slept.

A momentary disappointment slid through her, but the sensation was quickly erased by the blissful peace last night's lovemaking had left behind. Heaven knew she didn't have a lot of experience, but she couldn't imagine any other man igniting her senses the way Zach had.

He'd brought her to life—body and soul—as no one ever had before.

There had been one instant the night before, just before they'd entered the bedroom, when the logical side of her brain had almost regained control. Thankfully one look from Zach was all it took to convince her that making love to the man was not only what she wanted, it was what she needed.

Jess closed her eyes, picking up the sound of the shower running in the hall bath. If she wasn't mistaken, the tang of freshly brewed coffee had filtered out of the kitchen.

Jess smiled, tossing back the covers and easing her legs over the side of the bed. Her head protested slightly, so she sat still for a few moments, giving herself a bit more time before she stood.

Perhaps making love to Zach hadn't been the wisest move considering her recent head injury, but as far as she was concerned this morning, a few extra days of rest and recovery were a small price to pay for the intimacy they'd shared.

Zach had placed a pair of sweats and a robe next to the bed for her, and she gratefully snuggled into them, then padded toward the kitchen.

Jess paused outside the bathroom door, grinning at the sound of Zach singing in the shower. She pressed her fingers to her lips and laughed softly, then turned toward the kitchen and the promise of caffeine.

For the first time in her life, Jess realized she wanted to be with someone. Really *be* with someone.

That someone was Zach.

When he was by her side, she not only felt safe, she felt she could take on the world—and win.

Jess poured herself a cup of coffee, then headed out to the living room. Zach had told her about the police department's theory on Scott's death, and while she admitted the explanation made some sense, her gut wasn't buying a word.

Jess flicked on the television, hoping to catch news of the case, wanting to hear more details into exactly what the police thought had happened.

Instead shock filled her at the sight of a news crew reporting live from outside Whitman Pharma headquarters. She drew in a sharp breath and reached for the volume, turning it louder.

"The *Times Herald* alleges this morning that pharmaceutical giant Whitman Pharma has engaged in the tampering of clinical trial data in order to gain FDA approval for the much anticipated HC0815, touted as a side-effect-free cure for Hepatitis C."

Jess felt the blood drain from her face and she dropped her mug, sending hot coffee sloshing to Zach's carpet.

"Son of a—"

Zach's voice sounded from behind her and she spun on him. His dark eyes were huge and fury shone from their depths. "He gave me his word—"

"Who?" He'd told someone the details of what they suspected? After everything he'd said to her?

"Rick Levenson."

Zach gestured at the television set, hot color firing in his cheeks. "He said he'd sit on the information until I gave him the go-ahead."

"And you believed him?"

Zach shrugged. "I did, but maybe this is for the best."

She couldn't believe what she was hearing. "For the best?"

"This will force the whole issue out into the open."

She rubbed a hand across her face and blew out an exasperated breath. "*This* will destroy any chance of salvaging HC0815."

Disbelief twisted his handsome features. "Do you still think this drug isn't responsible for what's happened?"

Jess hesitated before she answered. "We don't have concrete evidence yet."

Zach stepped closer. "People are dead. Sometimes the evidence doesn't need to be neat and tidy and compartmentalized into tiny little boxes."

Heat fired in her cheeks.

"Sometimes things are messy," he continued. "Maybe you need to step out of the lab and look around you a little more."

"I gave Van Cleef my word."

Now it was Zach's turn to direct his anger at her. "You told Van Cleef?"

"I needed his help. *We* needed his help. I did the right thing."

"Did you?"

Jess rushed toward the door, reaching for her bag. She thrust Jim's rejected application into Zach's hand.

He stared down at the application, disbelief shimmering in his expression. "Why didn't you tell me?" he asked flatly.

"Because I didn't want to hurt you." Jess reached for the paper, slipping it from his hand. "I wanted to validate this first."

Jess's cell phone rang and she plucked it from her bag.

"It's a shame you didn't believe my threat." The voice from the street snaked into her brain, sending ice flooding through her veins.

She opened her mouth to speak, but fear squeezed at her throat.

"You've left me no choice."

The man disconnected before she could say or do anything. She pressed the menu button, retrieving the caller ID.

Unknown number.

Blocked.

Bile rose in her throat and she lifted her gaze to Zach's. "It was him."

He scowled.

"The man from the street." She swallowed, fighting the way the room had begun to spin. "My parents." Moisture gathered in her vision, blurring Zach's image.

"Jessica, I didn't know Rick would run with the story before I gave the okay."

"But you should have." She tucked the paper back into her bag and pulled open the front door. "Maybe you should start worrying about the living a bit more than you worry about the dead."

He reached for his keys. "Stay here. Please. You're safe here." He grasped her elbow and squeezed. "I'll call the station right now. I'll have a cruiser meet me at your parents. We'll move them somewhere safe. Just stay here."

Zach was in his car and backing out of the drive before Jess could say or do anything more.

"What have you done?" she whispered as he drove away. "What have you done?"

Chapter Thirteen

Zach downshifted and accelerated onto the exit ramp toward the Parkers' home. Jessica had phoned her parents and gotten no answer. The palpable terror in her voice when she'd called Zach's cell had been enough to make him regret ever sharing a single detail with Rick Levenson.

What had he been thinking? He might have talked a good game to Jessica about needing to let things get messy, but the reality was he had always been a stickler for procedure. Up until now.

Jim's death had tilted Zach's world on its axis, and nothing had been the same since.

What was it Jessica had said? He should start thinking less about the dead and more about the living? He shook his head, letting a bitter laugh slip from between his lips. She was right.

He snapped open his cell and pulled up the list of recently dialed numbers. He'd already spoken with his lieutenant. After taking an earful of reprimand and listening to the threat of suspension, Zach had been told backup units were on their way to the Parkers', but he still had one more call to make.

Levenson.

"Happy with yourself?" Zach barked out the words the moment Rick took the call.

"Matter of fact, I am. And you will be, too, once this thing breaks wide-open. I've already had calls from the Attorney General's office and the FDA."

Zach held the phone away from his ear long enough to scowl at the inanimate object, then he pressed it tightly to his face. "People's lives are in danger because of what you did."

"People's lives are in danger because of Whitman Pharma." Rick's voice boomed across the line. "At least that's what you told me. If you honestly thought I could sit on a story that huge, then you don't know me at all. I think you wanted me to do exactly what I did."

Zach winced at the truth buried in Rick's words. Part of him had wanted the reporter to run with the information he'd given him. Zach couldn't lie, not even to himself. He was tired of the investigation hitting one brick wall after another.

He'd wanted the dangers of HC0815 exposed and he'd wanted Whitman and New Horizon to pay.

He hadn't wanted to move before he could ensure the safety of Jessica and her parents.

"While you mull over that last thought," Rick continued, "there's been a new development."

Zach shifted his focus back to the call. "I'm listening."

"David Hansen's body was found this morning."

Zach's car swerved toward the shoulder, but he quickly regained control, working to wrap his brain around Levenson's words.

He was a no-show today. Jess's words bounced through his mind.

"Where?"

"In his garage. His ex-wife went looking for him after he failed to pick up his daughter for the weekend."

Anger and trepidation knotted in Zach's throat. "How?"

"Gunshot to the head. Coroner's office said he'd been dead at least twenty-four hours."

Zach's mind raced. Was there no limit to how far these people would go to hide the truth? Levenson was right. Maybe the article had been the only way to stop them.

Now Zach just had to reach the Parkers and get back to Jessica before the body count climbed any higher.

JESS HAD NO SOONER shut and locked the front door to her condo then she felt it. A presence. Something that didn't belong.

Check that. *Someone* that didn't belong.

She stood her ground without turning around, mustering every ounce of courage while simultaneously wondering if she could twist off the dead bolts and clear the front door before whoever stood behind her could stop her.

If only she'd done as Zach had asked—for once. She'd still be safely ensconced in his living room.

She reached for the bottom dead bolt.

"I wouldn't waste the time, if I were you."

Jess's insides rolled liquid.

She knew the voice instantly. Recognized it from her earlier phone call and from her earlier encounter with the man.

Her body began to tremble.

"You would have made my life much easier if only you'd heeded my first warning."

Jess swallowed, hanging on to the doorknob even as she pivoted, coming face-to-face with the man who had haunted most of her waking thoughts since she'd first seen him.

His hair was as perfectly coiffed as it had been the night he'd approached her outside. His suit the same sleek cut, although a different color and material. His eyes, however, had gone colder and more emotionless than she'd remembered.

Jess managed to force a single word past the knot in her throat. "Why?"

The man responded by stepping closer. "I could ask the same of you." He held up both hands and shrugged. "Why not walk away? Why pursue something you can't change?"

A frisson of bravery blossomed inside her. "What if I can change it? What if I set a process into motion that you won't be able to stop? No matter what you do to me."

He smiled. A cold, heartless smile that shook Jess to the bone.

"I've always enjoyed working with you idealists." He chuckled. "So refreshing."

The man took another step closer.

Jess pressed her back to the door, wincing at the bite of the doorknob as it dug into her hip.

"Who are you?"

"Let's just say we work for the same man."

Jess's mind raced, settling on the obvious choice. "Whitman?"

He laughed again and shook his head. "You truly don't listen well, do you?" He stepped closer still. "I said the same man. Not company."

Man?

Jess's stomach did a slow sideways roll. It couldn't be, could it?

Van Cleef?

"Ah, I see by your expression you've finally figured it out."

He pulled a gun from his pocket, aiming the gleaming barrel between her eyes as he tipped his head toward her bedroom. "Let's go. If I shoot you here, the bullet's likely to go right through that door."

Jess's mouth went bone-dry.

She hadn't come this far to have everything end like this, had she? If Van Cleef was to blame for everything—the fraudulent trial results, the deaths—she had to stop him.

She had to survive to tell someone the truth. To tell Zach the truth.

Jess studied the man, from his dead eyes to the gun in his hand.

How?

How on earth would she be able to get away?

She had to slow him down. Had to give herself time to think. Time to act.

"Did you break in the other night?" She asked the question without moving, holding her place in front of the door.

He nodded. "If I'd wanted to kill you then, you wouldn't have escaped."

Jess drew in a long, slow breath, willing her heart to stop pounding against her ribs. "And the fire?"

The man tipped his head from side to side. "I misjudged your ability to survive. His features brightened and he winked, the move in sharp contrast to his hard, scarred features. "This time I'll make sure you no longer have a pulse before I leave."

"What about my parents?" Her emotions knotted in her throat and her voice cracked on the last word. If this man had harmed her parents, she'd never be able to live with herself.

The man's features fell slack. "A convenient distraction. No doubt you sent your detective there, didn't you?"

She nodded.

"Do you see how good I am at what I do? Years of experience." He waved the gun toward her bed. "Now let's go."

Jess's relief at knowing her parents were safe tangled with the realization her own time was quickly running out.

"Someone will hear you, see you. You'll never get away with this."

Jess knew she was babbling now, but she didn't care. She refused to go down without a fight, and right now the only weapon she had was her ability to keep the man talking.

He made a tsking noise with his mouth. "Ms. Parker, you wouldn't believe the things I've gotten away with. As far as society is concerned, I'm invisible. That's what you don't understand."

He stepped close and tapped the gun against her shoulder. "Let's go."

Her trembling intensified and Jess's mind went blank. Except for one thought.

Zach.

He was the only person who might realize she'd gone to her condo, but that was only if he looked for her.

But he would. He had to.

He'd be calling any moment with word of her parents.

As Jess stepped away from the door and her would-be killer's gun pressed into her back, she could only pray Zach looked for her in time.

ZACH ROLLED TO A STOP in front of the Parker residence, pulling alongside a marked cruiser. He shouted through his already lowered window. "Any trouble?"

A young officer shook his head and gave the thumbs-up.

Relief surged through Zach, easing some of the dread he'd felt ever since he'd spoken with Levenson.

He parked the car, then pulled up Jessica's number on the cell, frowning when the phone rang several times and then went into voice mail. He'd have thought she'd snatch up the call knowing he'd be at her parents' by now.

Zach disconnected without leaving a message, then dialed his home number.

"Jessica." He spoke loudly after he pressed the key to bypass the outgoing message. "It's me. Pick up. I'm at your parents'." He paused for a few seconds but knew the machine would cut him off if he allowed too much dead air. "If you can hear this message, call me on my cell. It's urgent."

He waited for a moment before climbing out of his car, hoping she'd been listening but just hadn't felt comfortable answering his phone.

When no incoming call rang through, he redialed her cell, this time leaving a message there, as well. Maybe she'd just put down the phone and stepped outside.

But as he walked toward the Parkers' front door and the pair of officers talking on the front step, the tight dread Zach had felt upon receiving the news about Hansen returned, this time uncoiling inside him, spreading from muscle to muscle, bone to bone, until a chill raced up the back of his neck.

Something had gone wrong.

Dead wrong.

He knew it just as surely as he knew he'd fallen hard for Jessica and couldn't imagine life without her. Even if she had been so mad at him this morning he wasn't sure she'd ever speak to him again.

He'd given her his word that he'd make sure her parents were safe and hidden. He intended to keep that promise, but after he'd done so, he needed to track down Jessica.

Chances were she'd gone to New Horizon, ignoring his request to stay put—and safe.

Hadn't she mentioned something about needing to pick up the entry keys from her condo?

He might not be able to be in two places at one time, but he did know a way to clone himself, so to speak.

Zach snapped open his cell once more, this time phoning his lieutenant. Again.

The news about David Hansen's murder had apparently spread through the station. This time Zach encountered no criticism or reprimand.

"What's the address?" The lieutenant's question came without hesitation as soon as Zach asked that a car be sent to Jessica's condo.

Zach rattled off the pertinent details, including a description of the hybrid she drove.

"How soon will you be there?" the lieutenant asked.

Zach measured the lack of activity at the house and guessed Jessica's parents had already begun gathering their things. If they were anything like their daughter, they'd probably already had emergency bags packed.

He calculated how much time he'd need here plus the time needed for the return drive. Zach did the math in his head, then cut it by half.

Jessica's parents would surely understand if he kept the pleasantries brief.

"Forty-five minutes," he answered the lieutenant. "Hour, tops."

Then he patted one of the officers on the shoulder and stepped past him, into the Parkers' house. He only wished his visit were for a happier reason.

He could only hope that someday he'd get that chance.

JESS'S CELL PHONE RANG. Loudly. She'd left the volume on the highest setting so as not to miss Zach's call.

Her attacker's calm demeanor faltered momentarily, and the pressure of the gun between her shoulder blades vanished.

She spun on the man, swinging her bag—the bag he'd never asked her to set down—at his face.

The bag clipped his gun and sent the weapon clattering across her living room floor, but the man did little more than flinch. Then he lunged for her.

Jess was already in motion, racing toward the back of her condo but not knowing how she'd escape once she got there. Her assailant grabbed her by the hair and slammed her against a wall, sending crushing pain spreading through every inch of her already bruised body.

He threw her to the floor and she rolled, summoning up every ounce of self-defense training she'd had, moving out of his way just as he dropped on top of where she'd been.

He swore loudly and swung at her with his foot, clipping her in the shoulder blade.

Jess scrambled out of his reach, crawling across the floor military-style, fear and adrenaline tangling inside her, her mind suddenly razor-sharp, focused on nothing but survival.

She would not let this man win. Not now. Not ever.

She made it to the kitchen and scrambled behind the island, knowing exactly where she was headed. When he didn't come after her, she feared the worst. He'd gone for his gun.

He didn't disappoint.

"No matter what weapon you produce from behind there, you know what they say—" his bitter laugh sent the hairs at the base of Jess's skull tingling to attention "—scissors cut paper. Paper covers rock. Gun beats everything."

She took advantage of his bravado, easing open the oversized cupboard door beneath the island, knowing that—for the moment—she was completely concealed. She also knew she hadn't yet put a thing beneath the island, her cooking skills being rather limited.

She'd loved the look of the gourmet kitchen. She'd just never known what she'd actually use it for.

Until now.

Her attacker continued to talk, his voice grower nearer.

Jess backed into the tight space, crouched and ready

to spring. She pulled the door shut and waited, swallowing down the voice that nagged at her, telling her this particular idea was insane.

Considering there was only one way out of the condo, her plan might be insane, but it was the only one she had.

The man's voice went silent, then he laughed.

A deep, bone-rattling laugh.

"Honestly. Could you be any more ridiculous?"

Jess squeezed her eyes shut for a brief second, wishing somehow she'd wake up and this would all be a dream.

The tampered data. The suicides of Jim Thomas and the other students. Scott's death. The fire. Her attacks.

She wished none of it had ever happened. She wished she could go back to her life exactly as it had been.

Her belly twisted tightly in protest.

If her life were exactly as it had been, she would have never met Zach.

Her heart hurt.

Zach.

There was so much she wanted to tell him. So much she wanted to share with him.

She flashed back on the mind-numbing pleasure of their lovemaking and on how natural it had felt to wake up in the man's arms during the night.

"Come out, come out, wherever you are." Her assailant sang the words, taunting her, his voice coming from directly above where she hid.

Jess drew in a deep breath and focused.

Focused on seeing Zach again. Focused on surviving. Focused on bringing those responsible for the entire HC0815 fiasco to justice.

She pulled herself as small as she could, tensing her muscles and preparing to jump.

The cabinet door eased open.

The man's expression changed from smug to surprised as she hit him with her full weight, sending him crashing back on his heels, off balance and into the cabinets behind him.

He'd done exactly as she'd hoped. He'd squatted down to look for her, leaving himself vulnerable to her attack.

Maybe her plan hadn't been so ridiculous after all.

Jess scrambled around him, heading for the front door in an all-out sprint.

When a shot rang out, her insides caught and twisted, but she'd already undone the first dead bolt. With the second in her grip, she turned the lock and flung the door open in one smooth motion.

The doorjamb splintered beside her head, and she lunged into the hall, slipping on the tile floor as she raced for the front exit.

She slapped her palm against the intruder alarm and threw her full weight against the front door, tumbling out into the crystal clear October day.

The world around her seemed to move in slow motion, like a movie playing out on the big screen.

A man on a bike.

A young girl walking a dog.

The sound of children singing.

Her attacker's footfalls sounded loudly behind her and panic sliced through her. She fervently prayed he possessed enough humanity not to fire the gun into the peaceful Saturday morning, but she was wrong.

A shot rang out.

Children screamed.

Searing pain exploded in Jess's left shoulder, and she fell sideways, running into the street, focused only on escape and on drawing the man away from innocent bystanders.

She never looked down the street. Never saw the car coming. Never heard the rumble of the motor.

Her assailant caught her from behind and slammed Jess to the asphalt just as the approaching Cadillac caught the edge of her vision.

A massive car.

An ornate grille.

As Jess screamed in pain, fighting for her life, she recognized the driver's face.

The widow Murphy.

As she and her attacker wrestled in the street, the huge car bore down on them, seeming to speed up.

The driver's horrified expression was the last thing Jess saw before the moment of impact.

Chapter Fourteen

As Zach watched Jessica's parents drive away, police escort in tow, the full force of losing his own parents hit him, rocking him straight through.

He'd always known he'd stuffed down his grief, working to keep life as normal as possible for Jim.

But now…

Now the reality of being alone in the world hurt.

He smiled, thinking of the warm reception Jessica's parents had given him even though he knew full well they blamed him for setting today's events into motion.

Jessica's mother had hugged him.

Hugged him.

His throat tightened at the memory.

He never should have involved Jessica in any of this. He should have pursued the case and left her out of it. Instead he'd dragged her along for the ride, putting not only her life but those of her parents in jeopardy.

Jessica had been right—he'd been so focused on the dead, he'd stopped caring about the living.

As they'd said their goodbyes, the unspoken warning in Mr. Parker's eyes had been unmistakable.

Take care of my daughter. Or else.

Neither Mr. nor Mrs. Parker had voiced their concerns about their daughter, but Zach had promised them her safety.

"I won't let anything happen to her," he'd said in the moment before they'd pulled away from their home, headed into hiding.

"I know you won't, son," Mr. Parker had replied.

In the man's eyes, Zach had seen the same fierce determination and pride he'd seen in Jessica's each day since he'd met her.

He thought about how that look had softened during their lovemaking and about how peaceful she'd looked as she'd slept beside him, curled in his embrace.

He'd wanted to keep her there forever, inside his arms. Protected. Loved.

Loved?

Did he love Jessica?

He wasn't sure, but he knew one thing. Never before had one person come to mean so much to him so quickly. He wasn't about to lose her now.

Once they got past the resolution of the investigation, he'd make things right. He had to.

A uniformed officer tapped on Zach's passenger window, pulling his attention back to the present.

He leaned over to lower the glass. "What's up?"

The young man's brows furrowed, creasing his forehead. Zach read the look instantly, and a cold chill began to spread inside him.

Something had happened at Jessica's condo.

"We received a 9-1-1 from Ms. Parker's before we had a chance to get there."

Zach's throat squeezed. "And?"

"One body."

Zach fought to retain control, white-knuckling the steering wheel.

"Male." The officer glanced down at his notebook, then back at Zach. "In front of the condo."

Zach squinted. "Male?"

He drew in a deep breath, the picture of what had happened suddenly becoming crystal clear. The mystery man who had threatened her had made the call to her cell as a diversion.

He'd hinted at the threat to her parents, when in fact Jessica had been his target all along.

Zach bit back his anger at himself.

What a fool he'd been.

"Did they make an ID?" he asked.

"No, sir. The man carried nothing on his person."

So Zach had been correct. The man who had terrorized Jessica had been a pro—a hired pro.

"Apparently there was a scuffle in the street and an elderly driver hit the gas instead of the brakes." The officer made a snapping noise with his mouth. "Apparently the woman doesn't have the best driving record."

A scuffle?

"Jessica Parker?"

"No sign of her, sir. Officers on the scene checked parked cars within a three-block radius. No sign of the car you described," he continued. "Witnesses said the deceased had chased a blonde into the street, brandishing a gun."

"Gun?" Zach shoved a hand through his hair, biting back the sense of urgency that exploded inside him. He had to find Jessica and he had to find her now.

"One witness claims the woman was hit, but we weren't able to verify that. Apparently they tried to offer first aid, but she struggled free and ran away. The accident scene was pretty bad."

Zach leaned as close to the window as he could. "Did you check her condo?"

The officer nodded. "Door wide-open, sir. Definite signs of a struggle. We have a team there now."

"Do me a favor." Zach jammed the key into the car's ignition. "Tell them I said to check that gun against the Hansen murder."

"Will do." The officer lifted his gaze to Zach's, meeting his intent stare. "Do you have any idea of where Ms. Parker might have gone?"

Zach cranked on the Karmann Ghia's engine. "As a matter of fact, I do."

JESS PULLED TO THE side of the parking lot just inside the New Horizon gate. She'd tucked her car keys into her pocket before she'd entered her apartment. Without them, she'd probably still be running.

She'd heard the impact, heard her assailant's muffled scream, but then she'd heard nothing else. Somehow she hadn't been hit.

Commotion had broken out. Hands had reached for her, moving her, lifting her out of the street. Her neighbors had tried to help her, tried to get her to wait for medical assistance, but Jess had run.

She'd fled as fast as she could, blindly ignoring the pain in her shoulder. Ignoring the stain of blood blossoming on her shirt.

She'd never looked back. Not caring what happened to the man who had wanted her dead. Not wanting to ever see his face again.

Jess had never wished anyone dead, but there was a first time for everything.

Her only thought had been to get to New Horizon.

While she found it next to impossible to accept Miles Van Cleef had been behind everything, it made perfect sense.

She couldn't believe she hadn't seen the possibility sooner.

He had access to every facet of the database and coding system. He had a relationship with Whitman Pharma and with the local universities.

Miles Van Cleef had the ability to manipulate the system he'd created and hide every shred of evidence while he did so.

But why?

The man had been her role model—the epitome of a dedicated researcher. A man committed to finding cures for debilitating and fatal diseases.

What had changed?

She unbuttoned her shirt and eased the fabric from her shoulder. The wound still oozed but wasn't deep. Apparently the bullet had grazed her flesh. Nothing more.

She breathed a sigh of relief and reached into the glove box for the first-aid kit she kept there. She popped open the plastic container and pulled a handful of gauze pads from inside. She tore open the wrappers and placed the gauze squares on the passenger seat.

Next she pulled off several strips of medical tape, hanging them from the steering wheel as she worked.

Jess bit down on her lip as she pressed the gauze to the wound, working methodically to cover the bleeding, taping the edges of the pads until they were securely anchored to her flesh.

She gingerly pulled her shirt back over the dressing, refastened the buttons and reached in the back for the lab coat she'd left there the day before. It wasn't much, but it would conceal the bloodstain on her shirt.

Jess climbed out of the car and swore as she approached the front door to the building.

Her keys.

She'd never retrieved them from her condo.

How on earth was she going to get inside?

She scanned the parking lot for signs of other employee vehicles and spotted not a single one. She did see something else, however.

The fire-recovery company's van sat parked beside the side entrance.

Jess smiled.

Perfect.

ZACH RACED TOWARD THE New Horizon offices, pressing the Karmann Ghia to go as fast as possible.

"What do you mean there was no one there?" He hollered the question into his cell phone, shouting above the drone of the car's engine.

"No one but some recovery crew," his lieutenant explained. "Said they're working over the weekend to get the damaged lab up and running by Monday."

"So the unit left?"

Zach couldn't believe what he was hearing. The unit responding to New Horizon had simply driven away?

"There's no one else there, Thomas. No reason to stay."

"Well, can't they wait?"

"I'll have them loop back around every fifteen minutes," the lieutenant explained. "It's the best I can do. I can't afford to have that unit sitting in a parking lot waiting for something that might never happen."

Zach disconnected without responding. He was so angry his vision had gone red.

If his own police force wasn't willing to protect Jessica, he sure as hell would.

He wasn't surprised her car hadn't yet been in the lot.

The woman hadn't had time to make the drive cross-town. And if she'd been shot—Zach's stomach caught at the thought—driving would no doubt take far more effort than usual.

He glanced at the street signs as he flew past. Eight blocks. As he looked down the street ahead of him, he saw five traffic lights.

All red.

What he wouldn't give for his cruiser right now. There were times in life when lights and sirens really paid off.

This was one of them.

He approached the first red light and glanced in both directions. He could punch it across the intersection and miss the oncoming traffic by a mile.

Zach downshifted and smashed the accelerator to the floor. The Karmann Ghia gave a slight bounce as she cleared the side streets.

Not bad.

If the lieutenant wasn't willing to provide proper backup, Zach would kill two birds at the same time—getting police attention the illegal way and shortening his drive time.

He gave a tight smile and slowed at the next red light, glancing both ways before racing through the intersection.

He just might earn a police escort.

If he played his cards right.

ONCE INSIDE, JESS MADE quick work of Van Cleef's office door. The cleaning crew hadn't given her a second glance once they'd spotted her lab coat. She certainly didn't expect any further attention from them, and there wasn't another employee in sight.

Van Cleef typically left his office unlocked but hadn't this weekend. No surprise there.

She'd told him everything, for crying out loud. Zach had been right—she should have kept her mouth shut.

She could only hope Van Cleef hadn't taken the time to clear his office of any incriminating evidence.

She slid the plastic card for the employee parking lot gate along the seam between the door and the jamb, popping the knob on her second try.

Once inside, she closed the door behind her, assessing the office. Van Cleef's desk was covered by no less than eight stacks of papers and file folders. The credenza behind his desk was covered, as well, as was the far corner of the floor.

She'd always thought his system idiotic. Now she wondered if it wasn't in fact genius.

She decided to start with the desk, hoping anything as important as the master access key would have been placed there at some point.

She worked from left to right, front to back, sorting slowly and methodically.

She found nothing but staffing reports, schedules and out-of-date budgets until she hit the bottom of the fourth stack.

Disbelief knotted in her throat as she flipped through the document. Hadn't Van Cleef said he didn't know why the drug had been pulled from the pancreatic cancer trial?

She sank into Van Cleef's chair, tracing a finger down the columns detailing participant reactions.

They were ghastly...and deadly.

Zach had been right. The trial had resulted in two deaths. Both suicides.

No wonder the drug had been pulled from the FDA application process and no wonder Whitman had squashed all knowledge of these results.

Van Cleef had lied to her face and he'd done it well. Even though she knew now that he was behind the entire conspiracy, she couldn't quite wrap her mind around the fact he'd lied.

To her.

The mix of emotions tumbling through her went far beyond betrayal. They boiled down to a far more rudimentary sensation.

Pain.

"I had a feeling I'd find you here."

As much as Jess had hoped to hear those words from Zach right about now, it wasn't Zach's voice she heard.

"How could you?" Jess looked up from Van Cleef's desk, meeting her boss's direct glare. "How could you do this?" she repeated.

The man's glasses, as usual, were tilted crookedly on his face, but it was the expression in the eyes behind his glasses that turned her blood cold.

An expression she'd never seen there before.

Fury.

Blind fury.

She'd never seen the man angry, let alone livid.

And if she wasn't mistaken, the look in his eyes went far beyond livid.

The look in his eyes was downright lethal.

And intended solely for Jess.

Chapter Fifteen

Zach swore softly under his breath as he skidded to a stop next to Jessica's car. Not only was her car not the only vehicle parked in the employee lot, but her car's front seat was covered with discarded gauze bandage wrappers.

How badly had she been hit?

He glared at the car parked beside hers, shaking his head. Another hybrid. At least these scientific types put their money where their mouths were.

As he drew his revolver from his ankle holster and anchored it at the small of his back, Zach peered through the second car's windows.

Holy cow, what a mess.

The seats were covered with piles of papers and reports.

Zach straightened, searching his memory. What was it Jessica had said about Van Cleef? He preferred piles to filing cabinets?

If that were the case, chances were pretty good the second car belonged to Van Cleef. But hadn't Jessica said he never worked weekends? So what was the good doctor doing here today?

I gave Van Cleef my word.

Damn.

Zach winced and snapped his cell from his pocket.

Van Cleef.

The man had watched Jessica's every move from the beginning. Who better to know exactly what she'd been looking for and to whom she'd been speaking?

Scott McLaughlin.

David Hansen.

Both dead.

And who better to profit from the manipulation of a billion-dollar drug's clinical trial but the man who controlled how the trial was run?

Hadn't Jessica said his wife was very ill?

Well, Zach had heard of people who did far worse things to cover medical expenses or to provide for a loved one's care.

And Jessica had detailed every facet of their investigation for the man.

Trepidation twisted in Zach's gut.

His plan to draw a police escort had failed miserably. He'd blown past one cruiser, but his buddies probably thought they were doing him a favor by ignoring him.

Zach gripped his cell phone and punched the send key. This time when the lieutenant answered, Zach left no room for excuses. "Jessica Parker is inside New Horizon with the man we suspect of being behind most—if not all—of the cover-up."

"Your backup is five minutes out. Sit tight, Thomas."

But Zach already had his finger on the end button.

Five minutes was five minutes too long.

There was no way he was going to wait knowing Jessica was alone in there—alone with Van Cleef.

He was going in.

And he was going in now.

"I SHOULD HAVE KNOWN you wouldn't be able to walk away from a challenge," Van Cleef said as he stepped closer. "You never could walk away from a problem without working it to a solution."

He reached out and tapped his fingertip to the report. "If you hadn't met that detective, you'd have never known about this."

"Detective Thomas was approached by a consumer watchdog group." She looked up at Van Cleef. "They knew all about the earlier suicides somehow. Sooner or later they'd have gotten someone to listen or Zach would have found someone else to work with."

"Zach." Van Cleef pursed his lips. "So you and the detective are on a first-name basis?"

Jess said nothing, merely studying the anger shimmering in Van Cleef's eyes.

"Then you'll understand exactly why I did what I did," he said.

She shook her head. "I'll never understand why you would jeopardize a trial. Jeopardize *lives*."

"Love can make you do many things." His features softened. "Did you know our insurance doesn't cover my wife's inpatient care?" He thinned his lips, squinting. "You'll understand once your father is institutionalized."

Jess fought the urge to stand and slap the man. "Leave my father out of this."

"But you and I are the same," Van Cleef continued. "We know what it's like to watch a disease steal away someone we love."

Jess struggled to wrap her brain around what she was hearing. "What does your wife's Huntington's Chorea have to do with any of this?"

He smiled. "Money. In order to take care of her, I needed money." He shrugged. "Simple, isn't it? I suppose you wanted something exciting like corporate sabotage from a competitor, but the truth is just that. I needed money."

Jess pushed out of his chair, moving toward the door and her escape. Van Cleef's eyes had gone cold, and she needed to make her move now, while she had the chance.

She froze when he pulled a small pistol from the pocket of his jacket.

"It would be best if you sat back down." He waved the pistol at the chair.

Jess retraced her steps, lowering herself to the seat even as she processed possible escape routes.

The only way out was over—or through—Van Cleef himself.

Zach. Where was Zach?

She'd never checked her phone after it had rung, but she knew Zach must have been the caller.

He'd be looking for her now, wouldn't he? He'd have found her attacker in the street and he'd be searching.

Her gut screamed that Zach was on his way. She needed to keep talking. Needed to stall for time.

"Why HC0815?" Jess asked. "Why now?"

Van Cleef bit his lip, a flash of regret showing in his expression before he caught himself. "If you need money, why not go for the biggest drug ever to come down the pipeline?"

"Did you approach them or did they approach you?" Jess leaned forward, honestly intrigued to hear his response.

She needed to understand how someone as committed to the testing process as Van Cleef had come to prostitute the very system he loved—the very system he'd created to ensure the safe delivery of new drugs to the public.

His expression went smug. "I approached them." He waved the pistol, then retrained it on Jess. "Would you believe Blaire Wells knew nothing about the pancreatic cancer trial? Honestly, where do they get these people?"

Jess smiled, the move a bittersweet one. She and Van Cleef had shared the joke many times when speaking about marketing types.

She gave her standard response. "Who knows?"

Then she grew even more serious than before, her heart pounding so loudly she was sure Van Cleef must hear it. "What about the deaths, Miles? What about the students? The participants?"

"A necessary risk, I'm afraid." He shrugged slightly. "For others, HC0815 would have been a lifesaver."

"Would have been?" She seized on his word choice. "Do you honestly think it would have made it to market? Someone would have found out. You'd have never gotten away with it."

He shook his head. "That's where you're wrong. It was the perfect crime. Anonymous participants paid in cash. Suicides. Most families would be so encased in grief they'd never think to connect their loved one's death to the drug trial."

"Everyone except Zach." Jess pulled herself taller in Van Cleef's chair.

Van Cleef scowled. "You and that detective. The press is all over the story, even without proof." He inhaled deeply. "You've ruined everything."

"Then turn yourself in. Ask for a plea." Jess moved to stand, but Van Cleef waved the gun, gesturing for her to remain seated.

She did as he asked.

"If you turn on Blaire Wells, the authorities are bound to cut you a deal," she continued. "You know how it works, Miles."

He nodded. "I do."

"Then do it." She frantically worked to come up with

options for the man—options that would allow her to walk out of this office alive and bring him to justice.

"Tell me how you hid the data. Tell me who worked with you. Tell me everything. Then go into hiding and I'll work the deal for you."

Van Cleef's laughter started low, building to the most chilling roar Jess had ever heard.

A shudder ripped up her spine, spreading into her scalp and across her shoulders.

Her intuition began to scream.

But this time she didn't need intuition to tell her she'd sent the man over the edge.

When his laughter stopped, Van Cleef raised the pistol higher, pointing it at the space between her eyes.

"You have nothing to gain by killing me, Miles."

His brows lifted and he smirked. "At last, your methods of deduction are wrong." He took a step closer. "I have everything to gain. I'll have the satisfaction of knowing you didn't live to see the solution."

Jess watched as his finger moved against the trigger and she struggled to take in a breath, fearing the breath she took might very well be her last.

ZACH HEADED TOWARD THE building's side door, propped open, apparently by the work crew who had left their van parked along the curb.

He burst through the door, gun drawn. A handful of workers in protective gear froze where they stood, eyes growing wide.

"Police," he said softly. "Did a blonde come this way?"

No response.

"Did she?" he repeated.

Two nods.

"Little guy? White hair? Glasses?"

More nods.

Zach tipped his head toward the door. "Get outside and take cover. When the other officers get here, send them this way."

He could read the disbelief and hesitation on their faces. "Now!"

They moved, scrambling toward the door, each being careful to make a wide path around where he stood.

Zach worked his way down the hall, methodically moving past each office door, listening, gun held steady.

When he heard Jessica's voice, he hesitated momentarily, working to maintain calm.

"You have nothing to gain by killing me, Miles." Jessica's voice was sharp, clear, even though her terror was unmistakable.

Zach carefully placed one hand on the doorknob, keeping his gun held high in the other.

"At last, your methods of deduction are wrong." Van Cleef's voice sounded muffled, as if the man were facing away from the door.

Zach squeezed his eyes shut, trying to envision the scene inside the room.

Based on their voices, Jessica sat facing the door and Van Cleef stood facing Jessica.

"I have everything to gain," Van Cleef continued.

As Van Cleef continued to speak, Zach drew in a slow, steady breath and held it, praying he wasn't about to make a mistake that would cost Jessica her life.

"Miles, please."

The desperation in Jessica's voice grabbed hold of Zach's heart and squeezed. He shoved down the emotion and focused. He needed to draw on his years as a cop, needed to forget that he was more than likely in love with the woman on the other side of the door.

But when he eased open the office door and saw the stark terror in Jessica's eyes, all rational thought flew out of his head.

He moved quickly, silently, his eyes locked with Jessica's.

Van Cleef reacted to the change in Jessica's expression and spun on Zach, gun drawn.

The doctor was no match for Zach's training and experience.

In one swift move, Zach knocked the gun from Van Cleef's hand, sending it flying across the cluttered office.

Van Cleef paled as Zach trained his gun on the once-great researcher's face.

Zach gestured for the man to turn around. "It's all over. Hands on head. Move slowly to the wall."

Footsteps sounded behind Zach, but he didn't dare turn to see who approached. With any luck at all, the cavalry had finally arrived.

Relief flooded through him when he heard his partner Kevin Sweeney's voice. "Heard a rumor you were up to your old tricks. You never were a patient sort of fellow."

Zach stole a glance over his shoulder just long enough to see the other officer's grin. "And I see you're still taking your sweet old time."

Kevin shrugged with his eyes, then patted Zach on the shoulder. "I'll take it from here." He tilted his head toward Jessica. "Something tells me you've got other business to take care of."

Tears had begun to well in Jessica's eyes. She'd straightened and moved away from Van Cleef's chair, leaning her weight against the desk.

Zach reached for her, pulling her into his arms and out into the hall, as far away from Van Cleef as possible.

"You saved me," she said softly into his neck as he held her close.

"That's where you're wrong."

Zach pushed her out to arm's length and made sure she was looking into his eyes when he spoke.

"You, Jessica Parker, saved me."

They stared at each other for a long moment, then Zach lowered his mouth to hers, kissing her deeply, hoping the move would convey everything he didn't quite know how to put into words.

"I'm so sorry." Jessica's features crumpled. "I should have listened to you. I never should have said anything to him."

Zach brushed his thumb across her cheek, wiping

away the moisture, overcome with the depth of emotion swirling inside him. He shook his head. "You thought you were doing the right thing."

"And instead I tipped him off to everything we suspected."

"It doesn't matter now." Zach pressed a kiss to her forehead. "You're safe. Your parents are safe. That's all that matters."

He watched the sadness in Jessica's expression give way to relief.

"They're okay?"

He nodded.

RELIEF FLOODED THROUGH Jess, but suddenly she knew there was one more thing to be done.

If Van Cleef walked away now, they'd have only her word on his confession.

She wanted proof. Hard proof.

She twisted away from Zach and stepped back into Van Cleef's office. He'd been handcuffed, and the officers were just about to take him away.

"Where is it?" she asked.

The man she'd admired almost more than anyone else in her life lifted his defeated gaze to hers. "What?"

"You know exactly what." Anger began to edge out her disbelief. She knew precisely what she wanted and so did he. "The master access key."

The truth.

As the officers and Van Cleef brushed past her, he

uttered his answer flatly, under his breath. "File drawer. Left side."

"You filed it?" Jess asked, her voice full of disbelief.

Van Cleef shrugged. "I knew no one would ever look there."

Jessica watched as Zach stepped aside, letting the two officers take Van Cleef away. Then he returned his focus to her. She moved behind Van Cleef's desk and opened the file drawer, rifling through its contents without saying a word.

When her fingers hit upon the sheet of paper containing the information she and Zach had risked everything for, satisfaction began to simmer in her belly.

She held the emotion in check, knowing they weren't home free yet.

First the access key had to work. Then they had to hope it helped reveal not only participant identities but also the manipulation of the data itself.

"Well?" Zach's expectant question hung in the air as she pulled the paper from the drawer.

"Found it." She pushed out of the man's chair and stepped toward Zach, giving him a victorious smile.

She waved the single sheet of paper in front of his nose, then arched her brows.

"The access key?" he asked.

Jess nodded. "Let's go find some proof, shall we?"

TEN MINUTES LATER they were inside the system.

Zach had pulled up a chair next to Jess, and her

fingers flew on the keyboard. Nervous anticipation crackled in the space between them.

"There." Jess pointed to the screen as the list of files scrolled. "This has got to be the participant list."

She clicked on the file, entering the access key when prompted. She'd already used the key once in order to access the list of files.

She could say one thing for Van Cleef. He'd programmed layer upon layer of security into his treasured system. Realizing how proficient he'd been, she couldn't help but question whether or not HC0815 had been the only trial he'd sabotaged.

She shuddered at the thought, shoving the idea out of her head and narrowing her focus to the screen as a list of names and numbers appeared.

Zach leaned closer and Jess traced her finger down the screen.

"These are the codes randomly assigned to every participant," she explained. "They ensure the anonymity we promise to the participants and the drug companies."

"This—" she slid her finger to the right "—is the list of corresponding names. Maybe I can get this to sort alphabetically."

She manipulated a few of the database fields and smiled when the screen refreshed, this time displaying the HC0815 trial participant names in alphabetical order.

She read down the list silently, knowing Zach was doing the same over her shoulder.

"Mark Benton," she said softly.

"Amelia Grant. Roger Kowicki." Zach's tone had gone flat. "Son of a—"

"At least now their families will know the truth." Jess shot him a look and squeezed his knee. He lifted his focus to her momentarily, then turned his attention back to the screen.

She thought of his brother's application form, knowing exactly what was running through Zach's mind. Her heart beat a bit more quickly.

Please be here, she thought. Please. For Zach's sake.

She clicked on the mouse, moving down to the next page of names.

"Tracey Remington." Jess murmured the name as her eyes searched lower on the list.

There it was.

She blew out a sigh of relief just as Zach slammed his fist against the desk.

Jim Thomas.

Jess grabbed his fist, gently opening his fingers and interlacing hers with his. "We've got them now, Zach. Thanks to Jim and the others, we've got them."

Zach's throat worked and he stared at her intently. "How did they hide the reactions?"

Jess narrowed her gaze, studying the screen as she clicked the command to print the current report, then moved to a different list of files.

Once the participant report printed, she pulled the case reports for each of the victim's participant numbers, then waited for those to print, as well.

As she handed the stack of sheets to Zach, she formulated a plan in her mind.

"Why don't you read me each of those adverse-reaction codes—" she pointed to the appropriate space on each form "—and I'll look up what they stand for."

Zach started with his brother's report form, reading a series of three numbers.

"Headache. Nausea. Fatigue." Jess blew out a sigh. "It doesn't get more basic than that."

He then read Amelia Grant's form, then Mark Benton's. By the time he reached the fifth form, the pattern was blatant.

Each of the five suicide victims had identical adverse reactions listed. All of them anything but life-threatening.

"Now what?" Zach asked.

"Now—" Jess frowned, trying to remember where to find what she needed to find "—we see if management altered those numbers. When participants phone in their reports, the entry into the system is automatic, but if the reactions have been coded as something else, it's possible to control the results."

"Just like Scott McLaughlin said." Zach sat back against his chair, disgust and fresh grief plastered across his tired features.

Jess nodded, wanting nothing more than to hold the man even as she searched the management section of the New Horizon system.

"It has to be here somewhere."

She searched, flipping from screen to screen, menu

item to menu item. Suddenly there it was, buried in the study design section.

A few clicks later they had their answer.

Duplicate codes existed for the three adverse reactions reported, and when Jess traced them backward through the system, the original adverse reactions appeared on the screen.

Paranoia.

Depression.

Suicidal ideation.

Jess, shook her head, unable to believe her eyes. What was to stop another manager at another facility from doing the same thing to benefit another pharmaceutical company?

Van Cleef had buried the changes so deep within the system that no one would have ever found them if Zach hadn't pursued the truth. Once Scott McLaughlin was out of the way, only Van Cleef would have known the changes existed.

Zach tipped his chin toward the screen, his voice tight. "Print a few extra copies." He straightened, the muscles in his jaw working. "Van Cleef and his cronies might want copies for their scrapbooks while they rot in jail."

Epilogue

Jess stood back and watched as Zach pressed his fingertips to the bronze marker. The cemetery had installed it earlier that day, marking Jim's resting place.

Love and pride welled inside her as she watched Zach's broad shoulders hunched over his younger brother's grave.

She knew he'd be heartbroken over Jim's death for the rest of his days, but perhaps time would make the load easier to bear. And she planned to do whatever she could to make that happen.

The full investigation into New Horizon and Whitman Pharma had revealed that Jim and the other suicide victims had been placed on the highest possible test dose of the drug. Too much, quite obviously, for most healthy individuals' minds to handle.

Whitman and New Horizon had conspired to hide evidence, and innocent lives had been lost, all in a quest for riches and fame.

She blinked back the moisture gathering in her vision.

For the first time since she'd made her career choice, she was ashamed of her industry—an industry supposedly committed to finding cures, not death sentences.

When New Horizon had been shut down in a storm of scandal, Jess had lost her job along with everyone else on staff. Zach had suggested she start her own clinical trial company, and she'd actually considered the possibility for about ten seconds.

Then she'd decided this break was her chance to experience life a bit first. Zach had extended his leave, and they were headed out the next day to tour the country—one state at a time.

A bubble of warmth burst inside her. She couldn't think of anything she'd like to do more or anyone she'd rather do it with.

Van Cleef had given up Terrance Davis and Blaire Wells as coconspirators in the HC0815 scheme. In return, he'd been promised incarceration in a facility close enough to his wife that they might be able to see each other once in a while before her condition further worsened.

As Jess had suspected, the subpoena of Davis's financial records had shown regular cash deposits the authorities were able to trace back to the product development department at Whitman.

She shook her head. Not only had their greed taken lives, it had also permanently damaged the image of the industry in the public eye. Which, Jess thought, might not be an altogether bad thing.

Maybe the public could stand to be a bit more skeptical about new drugs before they rushed out to request them from their doctors.

Whitman Pharma stock had plummeted, and the FDA had launched a full investigation into every aspect of Whitman's organization and every trial ever run by New Horizon.

At last report, Whitman and New Horizon attorneys were working on an out-of-court settlement for the victims' families, but Jess had the distinct impression the families wanted to cause as much negative publicity for the companies as they could manage.

What better place to start than lawsuit after lawsuit?

The bottom line was that the truth had won out in the end.

Zach stepped away from Jim's grave and closed the space between them.

Jess reached up, pressing her palm to his cheek. "You okay?"

He nodded. "You know, that psychologist friend of mine said I needed to forgive Jim for dying." He tilted his chin toward his parents' headstone. "I was thinking I needed to forgive them, too."

"Then—" he drew in a deep breath and arched his brows "—I thought maybe the person I need to forgive isn't them at all."

"No?" Jess could feel her forehead crinkle.

Zach pressed a quick kiss to her lips, heating her instantly from head to toe.

"No." He smiled. "Maybe the person I need to forgive is me."

Jess blinked. "Maybe you need to stop feeling guilty for living?"

He nodded, interlacing her fingers in his. "I think I already have."

"I'm glad."

Zach dropped her hand and reached into his coat pocket, pulling out a long, thin jewelry box. Jess's pulse picked up a notch.

"For me?"

He nodded and pressed the box into her palm. "I thought you deserved a little something for all of your hard work on the case."

She laughed, lifting one brow suspiciously. She pulled the bow, freeing the ribbon and wiggling the top from the box. When she peered inside, she smiled with delight.

Jess lifted out the pendant—a perfect replica of the cheerleading trophy in her photo—and crooked her finger at Zach.

When he leaned close, she kissed him, then narrowed her gaze. "How did you get this so exact? It's identical."

"Well—" he wrapped an arm around her waist and steered her toward their parked car "—I know you don't believe in the whole photographic-memory thing, but I do have one."

"Zach Thomas." She wound her arm around his waist and pulled him close. "I believe many things now that I never believed in before, thanks to you."

He stopped walking, turning to face her. "Like what?"

She tipped up her chin and stared into his teasing gaze. "Like love."

He smiled down at her and, just before he closed his lips over hers, whispered, "Me, too. Me, too."

* * * * *

Turn the page for a sneak preview of
IF I'D NEVER KNOWN YOUR LOVE
by
Georgia Bockoven

From the brand-new series
Harlequin Everlasting Love
Every great love has a story to tell. ™

One year, five months and four days missing

There's no way for you to know this, Evan, but I haven't written to you for a few months. Actually, it's been almost a year. I had a hard time picking up a pen once more after we paid the second ransom and then received a letter saying it wasn't enough. I was so sure you were coming home that I took the kids along to Bogotá so they could fly home with you and me, something I swore I'd never do. I've fallen in love with Colombia and the people who've opened their hearts to me. But fear is a constant companion when I'm there. I won't ever expose our children to that kind of danger again.

I'm at a loss over what to do anymore, Evan. I've begged and pleaded and thrown temper tantrums with every official I can corner both here and at home. They've been incredibly tolerant and understanding, but in the end as ineffectual as the rest of us.

I try to imagine what your life is like now, what you do every day, what you're wearing, what you eat. I want to believe that the people who have you are misguided yet kind, that they treat you well. It's how I survive day to day. To think of you being mistreated hurts too much. If I picture you locked away somewhere and suffering, a weight descends on me that makes it almost impossible to get out of bed in the morning.

Your captors surely know you by now. They have to recognize what a good man you are. I imagine you working with their children, telling them that you have children, too, showing them the pictures you carry in your wallet. Can't the men who have you understand how much your children miss you? How can it not matter to them?

How can they keep you away from us all this time? Over and over, we've done what they asked. Are they oblivious to the depth of their cruelty? What kind of people are they that they don't care?

I used to keep a calendar beside our bed next to the peach rose you picked for me before you left. Every night I marked another day, counting how many you'd been gone. I don't do that any longer. I don't want to be reminded of all the days we'll never get back.

When I can't sleep at night, I tell you about my day. I imagine you hearing me and smiling over the details that make up my life now. I never tell you how defeated I feel at moments or how hard I work to hide it from everyone for fear they will see it as a reason to stop believing you are coming home to us.

And I couldn't tell you about the lump I found in my breast and how difficult it was going through all the tests without you here to lean on. The lump was benign—the process reaching that diagnosis utterly terrifying. I couldn't stop thinking about what would happen to Shelly and Jason if something happened to me.

We need you to come home.

I'm worn down with missing you.

I'm going to read this tomorrow and will probably tear it up or burn it in the fireplace. I don't want you to get the idea I ever doubted what I was doing to free you or thought the work a burden. I would gladly spend the rest of my life at it, even if, in the end, we only had one day together.

You are my life, Evan.

I will love you forever.

* * * * *

*Don't miss this deeply moving
Harlequin Everlasting Love story about a woman's
struggle to bring back her kidnapped husband from
Colombia and her turmoil over whether to let go,
finally, and welcome another man into her life.
IF I'D NEVER KNOWN YOUR LOVE
by Georgia Bockoven
is available March 27, 2007.*

*And also look for
THE NIGHT WE MET
by Tara Taylor Quinn,
a story about finding love
when you least expect it.*

HARLEQUIN® *Romance*®

presents a brand-new trilogy by

PATRICIA THAYER

Rocky Mountain
B R I D E S

Three sisters come home to wed.

In April don't miss
Raising the Rancher's Family,

followed by
The Sheriff's Pregnant Wife,

on sale May 2007,

and

A Mother for the Tycoon's Child,

on sale June 2007.

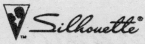

Silhouette®

ROMANTIC
SUSPENSE

**Excitement, danger
and passion guaranteed!**

USA TODAY bestselling author
Marie Ferrarella
is back with the second installment
in her popular miniseries,
*The Doctors Pulaski: Medicine
just got more interesting...*
DIAGNOSIS: DANGER is on sale
April 2007 from Silhouette®
Romantic Suspense (formerly
Silhouette Intimate Moments).

*Look for it wherever
you buy books!*